# THE DERIABAD CHRONICLES

# THE DERIABAD CHRONICLES

IRSHAD ABDULKADIR

PARTRIDGE

**To order additional copies of this book, contact**
Toll Free 800 101 2657 (Singapore)
Toll Free 1 800 81 7340 (Malaysia)
orders.singapore@partridgepublishing.com

www.partridgepublishing.com/singapore

For Amal, Zaynah, Laila, AIyaan and dear
comrade-in-arms, Aziz Sarfaraz

# Chapter 1

Sartaj was the eldest and should have been the leader of the pack. The mantle fell more readily on Meheryar's shapely shoulders. Behr-e-Karam was the third. A diplomatic little fellow who knew how to keep his half-brothers together or apart.

These were the princes, the sons of Ala Hazrat Nawab Sir Shahryar Alam Khan Umrani ruler of Deriabad State. There were lesser mortals too, sons of the palace doctor, a judge and a banker who participated in the recreational pursuits of the royals.

As long as they avoided restricted areas and interiors they were free to conduct their sporting activities in palace grounds. When they played cricket others joined in.

At Sartaj's suggestion they broke the rules at times and met after dark for hide and seek on roof tops amid the domes and turrets. Deriabad was … well … Deriabad.

One night they were caught scampering amidst domes by the sergeant of the guard. When questioned by the ruler the boys looked away, hummed and hawed, until Meheryar stepped up and claimed responsibility.

It remained that way through the growing years – school, university, military training course, internship at palace institutions, administrative duties of state into the grown up years. Complex assignments faced by Sartaj were invariably referred – at Sartaj's behest – to Meheryar, who reported back with solutions that were taken to be Sartaj's work.

The ruler suspected the truth but was loath to bring it up lest it struck at awkward issues like the right of succession. The princes, like well trained horses displayed no overt reaction to this. They had resigned themselves to the situation. Jobs assigned to Sartaj got done by Meheryar when the going got too tough for Sartaj.

In truth, Sartaj harboured a long standing resentment against Meheryar. His ability to best him at every turn was galling. His tall, physical beauty stood out in contrast to Sartaj's short, plump ungainliness.

Meheryar did not have negative feelings about Sartaj, but disliked some of his characteristics, and felt sorry for him. He realised that Sartaj was in an untenable position. He was not capable of dealing with matters of state that would come his way when he succeeded the ruler.

'He, will need someone to hold his hand and guide him.' Behr-e-Karam said, looking pointedly at Meheryar.

'Don't look at me … I'm just filling in for the present.'

'Who else Meheryar Bhai? … since the Deriabad establishment became a private enterprise, who else has the know-how, the way you do, of tackling our affairs? Even father turns to you.'

'So what?' How do you know whether Sartaj wants me to have any role in state matters while he doubts my motives.'

'Of you conspiring to take over the title?'

'Don't snigger,' Meheryar said, 'someone in the States and Frontier Regions Ministry sent me copies of letters he had written to the minister.'

'Whatever he says, he doesn't want you to go. He wants you to be near by for keeping an eye on you. Besides he recognizes your administrative skills and your powers of analysis. I heard him say so to father.'

'He praised me to father! You're making this up.'

'Minister Mehboob Alam Shah was present when he spoke. Ask him … he also commented on how committed you were to Deriabad and its future. Father heared him out, but all he said was that he hoped Sartaj and I had the same sense of commitment.'

Deriabad had ceased to exist as a princely state of British colonial vintage when the ruler acceded to the federal republic that came into being upon the Subcontinent's independence from British rule. The Treaty of Accession provided a special status with privileges to the ruler. It also made provision for the changeover of Deriabad from an independent princely state to an administered unit of the newly formed republic.

Despite the loss of sovereignty, Deriabad was well regarded. Its physical attributes included a terrain dotted with hills and fertile plains, a meandering river, a dam fronted lake, a desert, a pleasant capital city, the country's grain and cotton exchanges, a thriving industrial sector and a palace described as a forerunner of early 19th century Italianate style royal residences introduced to the Subcontinent. Deriabad also boasted architectural remains and antiquity sites representing the history of the Subcontinent. It was an important stopover in tourist itineraries.

When visitors called at Falaktaj Palace, the ruler frequently deputed Meheryar to take them around the palace and sites of interest in the city. He also assigned him to the capital on occasion for discussions at the ministry.

'He does it with such skill and finesse,' he mentioned to Minister in waiting, Mehboob Alam.

'He is aware of his facts and figures,' Mehboob Alam said, 'and doesn't give anything away.'

Everyone in the palace knew of the ruler's preference amongst the princes and expected *farmans* – royal decrees – pronouncing on succession, to be issued. The ruler had even discussed the matter with Badshah Begum – mother of Sartaj – who being an Umrani had listened stoically, with tears suppressed, to the ruler's plans for altering the succession.

'The Umrani legacy will survive if Deriabad's survives. With sovereignty gone and me gone, only an exceptional leader will be able to steer Deriabad in the right direction. I see that quality in only one of my sons. Do you want me to deny the Umranis the right to long term survival by giving way to the rule of primogeniture?'

But it was not to be. Out for a stroll one day with his dogs, the ruler had a stroke and the next day he was gone bringing Deriabad to a standstill.

His interment in the vaulted chamber of the royal mausoleum attended by high civil and military officials, local and foreign dignitaries and diplomats, gave rise to an unearthly chatter amongst nine generations of past Umrani rulers lying side by side.

'At last,' Greybeard said, 'a newcomer after fifty-five years'.

'Yes, great, great, great grandfather,' said Artful Arbab, 'he is my grandson, Shahryar.'

'What are you taking credit for?' Fussy Farhad remarked, 'We all know who it is ... everyone here is either someone's grandfather or grandson ... so why belabour the point?'

'I wonder.... I wonder', queried, Curioso, 'who has been named the alambardar – standard bearer.'

'Why should that matter to us?' remarked Grumbles, 'We're down here and that damned standard is for the living…'

'Still a matter of family importance', said Canny Kamran, 'especially since it is still missing.'

'Who cares…the Umranis are doomed anyway', said Grumbles.

'Stop you're chattering', snapped the Eldest Elder, anticipating Sufi Saeen's distress on account of references to the standard as it had gone missing during his reign, 'they're about to complete the burial ... standby to greet the newcomer'.

After the funeral - at which the ruler's titles and honours of state and of the British Empire were cited - the mourners returned to Falaktaj Palace, a three domed splendour on a parallel hillside overlooking the town. Three melon shaped dames adorned the front section of the palace. The rear portion with fountain centered courtyards and vast underground chambers, dated back to the 17th century.

Funeral feasts had been laid on four fifty foot long tables. One in the teak lined dining hall for family members and distinguished guests (including representatives of Queen Elizabeth II) and three in the palace gardens under a shamiana for the hoi polloi.

When lunch was announced, there was an unseemly rush to reach the table indoors. The entrance to the dining hall was jammed with bodies jostling and squeezing their way in. The frenzy was unabated within. Those who got through, raced to the table and loaded as much food as the crested plates could hold. Sterling silver forks and knives were used as weaponry to reach the dishes and were discarded soon after as bare hands proved better for seizing and devouring food. It was a far cry from the disciplined public feasts that had been held on Eid and Diwali during the long gone colonial *riyasat* days. But then most forms of behaviour were a far cry from the norms followed in earlier times. The free for all witnessed that day was symptomatic of prevailing national behavioural trends.

The last of the mourners departed as the evening shadows lengthened. Within the hushed interior of the brooding palace family members sat back in silent relief.

# Chapter 2

Allah Bakhsh poked and prodded a clutch of untethered buffaloes ambling in a wheatfield with his staff and managed to drive them into a cattle pen attached to his home. The quadrangular mud plastered structure stood amidst fields of stubbled wheat stalks some distance from Deriabad town in a rural settlement called Pattanwala.

The flickering flame of an oil lantern cast a wavering orange glow in the darkening courtyard. Charpoys set out for seating would later serve as beds. In the diffused lighting, Allah Bakhsh's eldest son Ameer Bakhsh, perched on a charpoy, pored over the contents of a candidature form for the forthcoming elections. On seeing him, Ameer Bakhsh jumped up with a greeting and fetched cold water for him in a clay bowl.

'Still wasting time fingering election forms,' Allah Bakhsh remarked.

'Who's wasting time, Abbaji?' Ameer Bakhsh said, 'you know I plan to stand for elections … for my future. Did you think I was going to serve the Umranis?'

'You know what I mean,' Allah Bakhsh said setting his staff and turban aside. 'Your future, hah! you think that will be better with the elections?'

'I'm as qualified as anyone else standing for election. At least I have studied for my degrees, not bought them.'

'Don't brag about your qualifications. Your education cost more than I could afford.'

'Abbaji, if I want to improve my life, why do you object?' Ameer Bakhsh protested, 'you know that in this country, there are only two ways to get ahead … by joining politics or by becoming an officer in the army. There is nothing your Umranis can give me.'

Their rising voices brought forth Allah Baksh's wife, Masuda Mai from the fireside where she was preparing the evening meal. From other rooms Allah Bakhsh's other children and Ameer Bakhsh's wife, Razia with a youngster in tow, emerged.

'You've lost your mind Ameer Bakhsh', Allah Bakhsh raged. 'Elections are fought and won by powerful people supported by big money and big influence of — of jagirdars, armed forces, mullas, businessmen and often the Americans. the rich, powerful people win — the same rich, powerful people every time. You are nothing before them.'

'I am not standing independently Abbaji, but as a party candidate. I have been given a ticket and the party will run my campaign'.

'Stop, your bickering', Masuda Mai yelled, 'morning, noon and night it goes on. Nothing else seems to matter to you two when there is so much more to be bothered about.'

'Listen to your daft son,' Allah Bakhsh said swatting a mosquito. 'He believes that the party led by that *Sona munda* – handsome lad – the retired Air Force hero, who has promised to turn the country upside down... is going to succeed against the parties who have always won elections.'

'Let him believe what he likes', Masuda Mai said dusting the flour from her hands. 'If he loses, it's not your turban that will fall'.

'You don't understand, you fool, that his party opposes the Umrani family who are our *mai-baap* – mother-father – whom we have served for generations'.

'In politics Abbaji, traditional loyalty gives way to principles based on what's right for the country'.

'You are saying that the Umranis who gave up their state to join the federation are wrong for this nation — without them there would have been no country. The Deriabad land mass is the vital link between the northern and southern federal territories. Without it, the country would be split with our land separating the two parts'.

'The state doesn't exist any more and national laws are binding on the Umranis. Gone are the days of nawabs and rulers.'

'Shut your mouth,' Allah Bakhsh yelled getting up in sudden anger to strike him.

'Will you hit your son over a silly argument?' Masuda said, rushing in to hold him back.

'The state will always be there.' Allah Bakhsh shouted. 'The Umrani family will always be our overlords. I will continue to serve them until I die, you damned traitor!'

'For God's sake,' Masuda Mai said, 'who's questioning your loyalty *saeen*? You are one of the most trusted *baildars*.

The Umranis rely more on your knowledge of titles to land and acre numbers than on the official revenue records maintained by *patwaris* and *tehsildars*.'

'You have spent a lifetime working for the Umranis, Abbaji, but that is not for me. I have given my time working for the welfare of my sector.'

'Welfare of your sector!' Allah Bakhsh said mockingly. 'You don't fool me. You picked up local NGO work which no one else would touch to get some recognition when you failed to get a city job even with your degrees.'

'That was because of my rural background … despite your Umrani connection, I was not considered good enough for those jobs.'

'Ungrateful wretch, all your life, you have benefited from the Umranis,' Allah Bakhsh said, 'this home, our small landholding, your education and marriage, all these were possible because of Umrani largesse. Only one year you have spent in social welfare work – the rest of the time you chased after that Air Force joker — and for this you have been given a ticket by a party that opposes our royal family. If you were that keen on being elected why didn't you try for a ticket from the National Front?'

'Because you have to be somebody before they look at you. Anyway, only corrupt persons and vested interests get those tickets. Besides, most of its tickets had been given to the Umranis or their supporters.'

'If you succeed, I wonder how you'll deal with corruption … will it still be service to self instead of the nation?'

After a pause, Amir Bakhsh said, 'You should know Abbaji … you raised me.'

The call for prayer forestalled further discussion. The men withdrew for ablutions and namaz while the women laid out the evening meal on a matted dais in the courtyard. Dinner was eaten in silence punctuated by the occasional chatter of the younger children and sounds of night creatures. Allah Baksh glowered through the meal. Ameer Bakhsh stared at his plate.

Afterwards Allah Bakhsh read the newspaper and smoked his hookah. His sons played cards and the women tended to the nightly requirements of farm animals before turning in. Some of the family members slept indoors while others preferred the courtyard under mosquito nets.

Ameer Bakhsh lay awake until midnight under an ink black sky studded with stars, disturbed by the unpleasant scene with his father. He tried fruitlessly to focus on the chores to be done for his political corner meeting. When that did not work, he awakened Razia and bade her follow him to the homestead roof. There they made love — fiercely at first, evoking a protest from Razia, subsiding gradually in keeping with the night's tranquillity. Aroused some hours later by the muezzin's pre-dawn call, Razia gazed at the square jawed handsomeness of her husband poised above her and let him go reluctantly.

Some distance away, in the palace, the ruler's French wife, Ninette was dreaming of the last time she lay in her husband's arms. Her maid tiptoed into her room. It was very late and most of the mourners had left. After the ruler's death, Ninette's situation had become somewhat uncertain. She would no longer be official consort.

That office would, upon Sartaj's assumption of the title of the nawab, devolve to his wife. Moreover, while the other begums, were viewed as ladies of significance in their own right owing to their family ties, this was not so in Ninette's case.

'No longer the favourite of the harem … the French connection is all she's left with', the maid overheard Sartaj's wife, Kulsoom mutter drawing smirks from her coterie. *Poor thing,* the maid thought, glancing at the sprawling figure lying face down on the gold leaf bed, limbs outstretched as if clinging to a life raft.

*What will become of all this?* she wondered glancing at the Louis XV bedroom suite and toilette table, the Savonnerie and Aubisson fittings, period paintings and objects d'art from Turkey to China assimilated painstakingly by the ruler for Ninette's chambers.

Two mini terriers peeped out from under the ornate bed.

# Chapter 3

Late at night, Sartaj Alam Khan waited at the palace with barely concealed impatience for the custodian of keys to the ruler's office to turn up. His half-brothers, Mehryar and Behr-e-Karam waited with him.

'Are you still heir apparent or ruler presumptive now?' Behr-e-Karam enquired.

'Don't know what the hell I am. I do wish that sodding key keeper would get here.'

'Easy Bhaijan, easy', Meheryar said. 'He'll be here, but what are you looking for in Ala Hazrat's office?'

'Direction, Lady Ninette mentioned that he had left some guidelines.'

'Guidelines for an occasion like this?' Meheryar asked, brows raised over luminous eyes so reminiscent of the ruler.

'I don't know about what occasions, but Lady N said that they were to be read out after his death.'

'Oh, yes,' Meheryar said, 'now I recall her mentioning them. You're right Bhaijan, this is a good time to read them.'

Just then two state officials came into the ante-room, somewhat out of breath.

'Ah, the white rabbit himself,' said Behr-e-Karam, referring to the custodian of the keys.

'Accompanied by the Mad Hatter', Meheryar muttered under his breath, referring to the minister in waiting, Mehboob Alam Shah.

'You've kept us waiting, Hamid Ali', Sartaj said scowling.

'I'm very sorry Prince, but I had to find Shah Sahib.'

'Why?'

'Because he has to be present when keys kept in custody are used to open sealed apartments'

'He's only observing correct procedure, my Prince', the minister said.

'Very well. Get on with it,' Sartaj said.

The custodian drew out a bunch of keys from a leather pouch and unlocked the office door. The ornate panels swung open on a dark interior into which the minister proceeded followed by the princes.

'Open sesame,' said Behr-e-Karam with a chuckle.'

The custodian fumbled briefly at a switchboard, managing at last to turn on the wooden chandelier that hung from the centre of the ceiling like a corona of branching wild buck horns. The wood panelled room was divided into an elaborately furnished sitting area and an office section with desk and office table equipment for the ruler's use surrounded by portraits of past rulers in ceremonial dress.

The princes were hesitant not knowing what to expect. The minister of state paused before speaking, 'I assume my Princes, that you are here to ascertain Ala Hazrat's views on the running of state affairs after his death.'

'We were told that he had left some instructions', Sartaj said.

'Ah yes, he did', the minister said, 'but they were to be read out before the principal groups of the family'.

There was another pause, glances exchanged, uncertainty writ large on most faces.

'I think all who matter are present here', Sartaj said firmly. 'I represent Badshah Begum, Prince Meheryar is Rani Sahiba's representative and Prince Behr-e-Karam speaks for himself.'

'What about Her Highness, Lady Ninette Sahiba?' the minister asked. The princes looked at each other.

After a while Sartaj mumbled 'She won't come … she's in mourning. I will represent her and also the orphaned princesses.'

'I suppose — I suppose that should be in order', said the minister, looking around nervously.

'It'll have to be, Shah Sahib', Sartaj said sharply.

'Excuse me,' Meheryar interceded standing up. 'That doesn't seem right. All concerned family members should be present. Sorry Bhaijan, but any other way could be challenged by those left out.'

Sartaj grimaced, at a loss for words. Finally, he grunted, 'Okay okay … but how are we to get Lady N to attend?'

After a whispered consultation between the minister and the custodian, the minister suggested that Meheryar and Behr-e-Karam should approach her. At Sartaj's insistence this was done despite the lateness of the hour.

A sleepy Ninette signed an authorisation for herself and as guardian for the minor princesses for the reading of the late ruler's instructions despite their absence. It was almost morning by the time Meheryar and Behr-e-Karam returned with authorisation in hand.

The minister rummaged for another set of keys and opened a central drawer from which he took out a silver box inlaid with gem stones. Another key opened the box. A sealed off-white cover with 'To be opened after my death', inscribed on it bearing the ruler's signature, lay on top.

'With your permission, my Princes', the minister said flicking open the seal and drawing out a document written in the ruler's inimitable hand.

'Read it out', Sartaj said.

After clearing his throat, the minister read, 'Beloved family members: I leave here a few words for you to ponder over after my death.

The sovereignty of our state is merged with the federation, and, as you are aware the family has been granted a special status on account of the merger, which entitles its members to several privileges. Despite the absorption of Deiriabad's sovereignty, there is a royal establishment with properties and interests (hereinafter called the 'establishment properties') that continues to exist and will devolve upon each succession to the next ruler. There is also the institutionalized status of Deriabad which has been preserved by succeeding rulers. So long as this tradition is followed, the entity will survive. There should be no question raised on this account. The establishment will devolve to whoever the federal government recognizes as the next ruler.'

'Little doubt on that score', Sartaj grunted.

'There is more', the minister remarked. 'May I continue?' 'Go on', Behr-e-Karam said.

'The list of establishment properties with fixtures, fittings, furnishings, household items and spare parts in storage which accompany this title is set out in Schedule A. Most of these properties are known, but some here and abroad may not be in general awareness.

The state jewellry which is listed in Schedule B, will devolve to the custody of the next ruler.

The state weaponry, vehicles, implements, mechanical devices, stores, granaries, animals and all other objects, items and effects of general use listed in Schedules C, D, E, F and G will remain with the establishment.

My personal effects, garments, jewellry, prayer books, rosaries, prayer mats, bank accounts, objets d'art, books, correspondence, photographs and gifts received, all as listed in Schedule H, are bequeathed to the persons mentioned in the table of bequests attached to Schedule H.

Office correspondence, Deriabad State bank accounts and balances, policy and administration paraphernalia will be taken over by my successor.

Finally, the office of the standard-bearer, the alambardar, the precedent of the alam's custody devolving to the succeeding ruler will not be followed on this occasion.'

All present gasped and Sartaj looked stricken.

'Whoever finds the alam and brings it back to Deriabad will be the next alambardar. The survival of the institution of Deriabad is contingent upon the recovery of the alam.'

'That could be anyone, even a stranger,' Meheryar interrupted, hinting at the possibility of the alam passing to an outsider.

'Anyone' the minister repeated, 'Ala Hazrat sought to separate the spiritual legacy from the temporal, by this move'.

'But', sputtered Behr-e-Karam, 'the alam has been the symbol of sovereignty ever since our ancestors staked a claim to territory in the Subcontinent under the suzerainty of Mohammad Bin Qassim.'

'Not quite, Prince Behr-e-Karam. After the conquest of Sind, the alam was installed at the head quarter of the first Umrani affirming allegiance to Islam in a land of idol worshippers,' said the minister. 'But it was intended to be an institutional emblem not a royal one.'

'Doesn't matter what it was meant to be,' Sartaj said, walking round the ruler's office table petulantly, 'I know why father has done this... he wants to cast doubt on my accession'.

*Serves the buzzard right,* thought Meheryar. *Wants to grab everything.*

The silence that followed the remark was interrupted by a polite cough from the minister.

'Prince Sartaj, you are the next head of the family and will be installed as nawab. The federal government will see to that, I'm sure'.

'There will always be questions about my right to rule', Sartaj said grim faced.

'Rule, what?' Behr-e-Karam murmured inaudibly, 'the state's gone for good... all that's left is the title and a tottering establishment... rather like a hollow crown.'

'What's that?' Sartaj enquired.

'Nothing...nothing important,' Behr-e-Karam said winking at Meheryar.

But there was something of importance to consider ... Meheryar looked out of a window at the morning lighting up yellow mustard blossoms dotting cultivated fields.

*I am not going to oppose him, for the sake of opposition. So no threat there but if I decide to continue working for the palace, it will be on my terms. Whether I work at the palace or elsewhere ... if I find that he is riding roughshod over Deriabad interests or that his policies are damaging the palace or harming family interests ...I will move ... won't let him destroy what the Umranis have built ...*

When Meheryar turned away. The early rays of the sun were touching the tops of ripening crops.

A dirt track between the fields ran alongside a waterless irrigation channel lined with chocolate coloured clay caused by sporadic flows of water. Ameer Bakhsh rode his motorcycle roughshod over the track. It threw up powdery vapours of dust when encountering runnels – and embankments.

He was unmindful of the discomfort suffered by the pillion riding *patwari* each time the motorcycle ran into impediments bringing the latter's pot belly smack up against Ameer Bakhsh's sturdy back.

He was in a hurry to get to Deriabad town for filing his candidature papers before the election commission office closed for the day. The *patwari's* presence, in the capacity of a revenue department official from Ameer Bakhsh's locality was necessary for verifying Ameer Bakhsh's statements on the forms. Ameer Bakhsh's advocate, who was to be the second verifier, awaited them at his chambers adjacent to the court. The town notary also awaited them. He would be called upon to attest the signed documents.

Hours later when Ameer Bakhsh had completed the requisite steps, he was stopped from entering the election office by a burly ranger on duty.

'Why are you standing in the way?' he enquired.

'You can't enter while the Umrani Princess Bisma Sultan is inside filing her candidature papers.'

'Princess Bisma Sultan, filing candidature papers so soon after her father's death!'Ameer Bakhsh remarked, then without waiting for comment, 'anyway this is a public office and all citizens have right of access without hindrance.'

'May be so in the cities,' the ranger said twirling his moustache,'it's different here when a royal lady is present.'

'The royal order finished when the state became part of this country,' Ameer Bakhsh said with rising indignation.

'Royalty is royalty, state or no state. Purdah has to be observed when royal ladies are present. Now stop bandying words with me or you'll have to move,' the ranger said stroking the butt of his shotgun. Ameer Bakhsh was about to challenge him but was restrained by his companions.

Half an hour later as the muezzin's call for the evening prayer rang out from the central mosque, Princess Bisma, attired in mourning black, veiled and surrounded by a small entourage was ushered out of the election office with great deference by the incumbents. They escorted her to a waiting Mercedes-Benz, bearing a Deriabad state number plate. A junior official held the car door open. A whiff of jasmine floated in the air as she passed by a glowering Ameer Bakhsh. After the car had driven away, the election office closed for the day. The officials streamed hastily across a roundabout to get to the mosque on the far side.

The guard shrugged his shoulders grinning at Ameer Bakhsh, who cursed, spat on the ground and spun the motorcycle round.

# Chapter 4

The mourning lasted for three days. In the ladies' section of the palace women callers shoved and pushed as belligerently as the men. The flag of the federation flew at half mast signifying a national loss. Two dogs in the palace kennels, a cocker spaniel called Alpha and a retriever called Arrow, were among the genuine mourners.

In a large hall fifty-four year old Badshah Begum, the first lady of the harem held court over a sizable gathering of women. She was an Umrani by birth and the ruler's cousin. Tall, imperious and formidable, her stance and style denoted her lineage. She did not suffer fools lightly and was occasionally disdainful towards the other Begums, acknowledging their presence as a necessary aspect of the royal tradition of co-wives.

A smaller group of tribal women chanting a dirge in their dialect, had gathered around Rani Satrangi who was an aristocrat in her own right. She was in her early fifties. Her father was Raja of the Hindu tribes of Satrang, a desert region in Southern Deriabad. Her ancestors had preceded the Umranis as overlords of the territory that subsequently comprised Deriabad state. Their presence in the town was signified by a district called Satrangbela. Rani Satrangi was born and raised in her family haveli in Satrangbela.

Glowing olive skin, fierce black eyes, aquiline nose and widespread cheekbones were the hallmarks of Satrang handsomeness. Rani Satrangi's two children, Princess Bisma Sultan and Prince Meheryar had inherited these attributes.

Having spied her accompanying her father on a flight from Deriabad to the port city, the ruler succeeded in persuading the aging Raja to accept his marriage proposal in preference to offers from Hindu royals in the neighbouring country

The Rani had accepted Islam as a precondition to marriage with the ruler. The alliance was regarded a political move — reminiscent of the Akbar-Jodha Bai union — deemed essential for fostering peaceful co-existence between the thirty-five percent Hindu with the fifty-eight percent Muslim Deriabadis. In private moments, the Rani kept face with the Hindu pantheon of gods and observed the annual Saraswati Puja. On formal occasions, such as the funeral, Rani Satrangi donned the traditional Cholistan attire: *ghagra, choli* and *orhni*.

There had been three other ladies. One, the ruler's cousin from a branch of Umrani kinfolk based in the neighbouring country. She gave birth to Behr-e-Karam, the third son of the ruler. Later, she was killed in a car crash. Another lady, also deceased, was the mother of two princesses.

The two princesses, Sadia Sultan (Sadie) and Rabia Sultan (Rabby) were twins. They were barely two years old when the ruler brought home a French bride fresh from Paris who, without having been forewarned of their existence at the time of her marriage to the ruler, took them over as surrogate mother.

Many saw this as a classic rehash of the union of the oriental potentate and the white maiden — a recurrent theme since the time the colonized developed a yearning for the colonizer's keep, but it was not quite so. Ninette de Villemoran bumped into the ruler at a stamp auction in Paris. They were both interested in acquiring the same stamp. He withdrew his bid when he learnt of her offer. In gratitude, she invited him to lunch. The luncheon episode was pleasant enough to lead to another, and another during the course of which they discovered love for each other. With her interest aroused, she researched Deriabad and the Umranis.

The initial shock of the multiple wives wore off when she realized that his life had followed the traditions of his birthplace and learnt of the circumstances of each marriage.

At twenty-seven Ninette was fourteen years younger than the ruler. She was single, blonde, attractive and reasonably well off. She owned an atelier which catered to the requirements of well-heeled country gentry. She was prepared to give it all up to be with the ruler.

There were offspring from four of the marriages. Ninette was childless. She had undergone two life threatening miscarriages before deciding to forgo pregnancy. Instead, she consoled herself with her surrogacy.

Badshah Begum's only child, Prince Sartaj Alam Khan, was the heir apparent. At thirty-four, he always seemed to be waiting in the wings. A passing resemblance to his mother was his only claim to Umrani looks. Unlike his father, he was short statured, rounded, receding chinned and balding. Sartaj lacked leadership qualities. He had little learning, limited vision and lacked competence. He had been a disappointment for his father. He was a disappointment for his mother too, but she would never admit that.

She realised that she had to stand by him in all circumstances. To buttress his position she had insisted that he retain Meheryar (with full powers) as Chief Advisor. Sartaj was initially reluctant to do so, but realized somewhat grudgingly, that it was the right thing to have done, since Meheryar virtually ran the state.

In the darbar hall, he stood at the head of a reception line of nawabzadas lined up in hierarchical order, shaking hands with or embracing callers. Next to him was Meheryar, imposing in black and next to him, Behr-e-Karam.

Among the women mourners, Sartaj's elephantine wife Kulsoom, was firmly grounded in a group of ladies surrounding her mother-in-law, Badshah Begum. Her massive buttocks occupied the space of three women joined at the hip. Her cries overrode the sound of the wailing women causing Badshah Begum to wince every time the decibels rose.

Badshah Begum rued the day when despite the family's advice to the contrary, she gave her consent to the marriage of Sartaj with Kulsoom. Bitya, as she was called at the time was adept at wheedling her way into the palace when her father came to tutor Sartaj in Quranic studies.

During recess in the tutorials she flirted with the simple-minded boy to such extent that he believed he was in love with her. After that there was no way back. Sartaj's mulishness wore down his father. Insofar as Badshah Begum was concerned, Kulsoom's single-minded devotion to Sartaj convinced her that her presence in his life would catalyse his transformation into a prince worthy of the ruler. It did not work that way. The emblem of hope became the proverbial millstone before the henna had dried on her hands.

Badshah Begum found it hard to overlook the squalor wrought by Kulsoom's grubby kith and kin squatting in Sartaj's house. Now whenever she thought of Kulsoom one word came to mind: blight. She felt that Kulsoom had been sent as a blight on the Umranis. Her aversion extended to Kulsoom's sons too and to everything associated with her. Blighted off-spring of a blighted mother was how she saw them.

After the funeral, Rani Satrangi's daughter, Princess Bisma Sultan, tall, stately and beautiful, flanked by the two flower-like princesses, Sadie and Rabby, stood at the main door of a hall leading to the grand staircase, seeing off departing visitors.

For Ninette there was a sense of having been cast drift by the ruler's death, but inborn Gallic realism had prevailed. She aimed to retain her privileged status and to continue relying on the family connection, but staying on in Deriabad was not viable as her link with the place was severed, and a royal dowager's existence in an ex-princely state of which she was not a native was a dead end. Life with her parents was also not an option, as she had outgrown provincial France. Paris however, was another matter as was the cosmopolitan port city, which served as a watering hole for Umranis travelling away from or returning to the country. The latter was an expedient choice, she reasoned, which would enable her to retain a link with her marital home.

She decided that the princesses would continue to live with her until they got married. Ninette's plans had always included the princesses. The ruler had given them to her on her first day in Deriabad and she had held on to them. They were regarded as much part of her brood as the other royal offspring were of their natural mothers.

'Listen darlings,' she said to them, 'now that your father has gone, I'm going to leave Deriabad and make a home for us elsewhere.'

'Where?' the girls asked, eyes wide with concern.

'Well, the port city for one – six winter months there with visits to Deriabad and the summer months in Paris and other parts of France.'

'Great,' said Sadie.

'We'll move into Deriabad House at the port city soon.'

Despite the pall of the mourning period, Meheryar decided to get back to work. 'The best cure for a grieving heart,' he had been advised. He was in the throes of a deep depression caused partly by the unexpected loss of his dear father, and partly by the uncertainty of the affairs of state. Now there was no one at the helm of affairs, no steady hand on the till, no clarity on whether the Deriabad administration would continue as before or be shuffled. He regretted being passed over but realised that underlings must follow the ordained course.

*That's what Providence decided, he* mused. He was not sure whether Sartaj would remove him from the post of Chief Advisor to the ruler, but shrugged his shoulders and laboured on gamely.

In contrast to this, Behr-e-Karam felt he stood on a better wicket with Sartaj as Captain. There would be more room for manoeuvrability between half-brothers to achieve his aims. Besides, having canny Meheryar as head of the household would have been a major impediment for putting into effect schemes he had been working on which required using state resources to further his personal objectives.

# Chapter 5

At the federal capital, Javed Rizvi, a section officer at the Ministry of States and Frontier Regions was trying to sort out the Deriabad files in the presence of a Major Tariq from the Quarter Master General's office at the GHQ accompanied by other military personnel representing secret and security services and bureaucrats from departments connected with Deriabad State matters.

Since the ruler had not named his successor, they had come together to discuss the issue. The younger officials mentioned the preferences of their departmental heads on the choice of the successor. The senior officials maintained a neutral stance. While Javed Rizvi voiced the federal government's support for Sartaj for the office of the nawab, the majors aired the preference of their respective agencies for Prince Meheryar, the second son of the ruler.

The political implications from the government's perspective of both options were taken into account. Javed Rizvi pointed out that although Meheryar was clearly a better choice, he was shrewd, very much his own man and prioritized Deriabad interests above others, while Sartaj was a plodder 'who could be led by the nose from point A to B without tipping the scales.'

Details of the three hour long discussion were minuted and dispatched to decision makers in the ministries, the GHQ and the agencies. The decision on the succession ultimately turned out to be no more than a white paper exercise. In the final round, the GHQ and the agencies in deference to factors such as real politik and primogeniture threw their lot in with the ministry. That is how Sartaj succeeded his father.

The Deriabad citizenry was not cheered by the news. It knew that Sartaj was a weak-kneed bumbler, mean tempered and melancholic. That the power, such as it was, would be exercised by Kulsoom, who, having risen from the rank of a cleric's daughter to become consort of her father's royal pupil, had the makings of a nascent power house.

The *gaddi nashini* which entailed Sartaj's 'enthronement' was a lacklustre affair. It took place after Friday noon prayers in the palace grounds. It was attended by male members of the Umrani family, state, provincial and federal officials, GHQ representatives and the local gentry. After Quranic recitations and all too familiar speeches from official and familial sources followed by a desultory response from Sartaj, the *dastarbandi* was performed by the state senior minister, who fidgeted long and hard with the turban material that had to be wound round Sartaj's head before he could ensconce himself in the gilded chair.

One by one the princes offered Sartaj allegiance. He nodded acknowledgment en passant and led the gathering to the buffet tables amidst cascading rose petals.

At a family lunch hosted by Rani Satrangi a few days later at Do Minar Haveli, Bisma and Meheryar chatted about the *gaddi nashini* in hushed voices to avoid being overheard by the twin princesses who were also present.

Their tete-a-tete was interrupted by Rabby.

'Meheryar Bhaijan,' she said, 'can you tell us about the disappearance of the standard.'

'That's a tall order,' Meheryar said with a dimpled smile.

'Please, please, please,' Sadie remarked, 'its an important part of family history, and we know so little about it.'

'Very well,' he said resignedly. 'The standard disappeared during great grandfather's time'.

'Sufi Saeen, wasn't it?' Bisma asked, 'I heard it happened during a spell of transcendence he experienced'.

'Nothing of kind', Meheryar said with a short laugh, 'he was zonked out of his mind — when he came to the standard was gone and in its place there a topknot of grizzled white and grey hair chopped from a scalp.'

'Meheryar, that's not what his half-brother reported. Faqir Bande Nawaz's account dismissed the charge as calumny spread to cause trouble',Bisma said.

'Believe what you like, Apa', Meheryar said. 'I have my doubts about Sufi Saeen's saintliness. The fact is, the standard disappeared under his nose – and there's no explanation, no accounting, nothing. It was a holy standard signifying victory for the Muslims in setting up a base in the pagan Indian Subcontinent, forever lost to posterity because of his so-called transcendence.'

'He walked barefoot throughout the state seeking people's forgiveness, often breaking into tears. He went into mourning for the remainder of his life', Bisma said.

'A ruler weeping in the market place — what better spectacle could the people want', Meheryar said.

'You're quite horrid', Bisma said smiling wryly, 'such cynicism about an ancestor who is revered by ordinary folk to this day'.

Rabby and Sadie, who had been listening intently took up the refrain playfully by crying, 'Traitor! Traitor! Mehryar Bhai is a traitor ........'

'Lock him up in the dungeon at the fort', Rabby yelled.

'Off with his head,' Sadie cried.

'Who's baiting who now?' Meheryar called out good naturedly, dodging the cushions Sadie slung at him while Rabby came to his defence by putting her arms round him

'Careful with your aim, otherwise you'll knock down a lamp,' Rani Satrangi warned as she came into the salon.

'Weren't there extensive searches made for the standard from time to time?' Bisma enquired.

'Yes', Meheryar said, 'both grandfather and father had statewide searches for which even the British resident sent search parties, but no standard — to this day'.

'We heard terrible consequences were forecast if the standard was not found', Sadie said.

'That's right', Meheryar said, 'Faqir Bande Nawaz writes about three mendicants appearing mysteriously in different parts of the state predicting doom for the Umranis'.

'How awful', Rabby remarked.

The younger Umranis listened raptly to this discussion on a matter of family interest. Meanwhile Meheryar scanned a written account of the event in a book — drawn from a shelf — on mysticism and mysteries of the Subcontinent by Ambrose Patterson.

'One of these harbingers of doom was called Naag Baba — ominous sounding name. He went about reciting Quranic passages — aptly or inaptly, as threats — to drive home his point.'

'What were these threats?' Rabby asked.

'Enough', said Bisma 'it makes my skin crawl to hear them'.

'We want to hear about it', Rabby said. 'No one has told us the whole story. Bisma Apa, you don't mind do you?'

'O well, go ahead, they may as well know.... but leave out the blood and gore'.

'The second chap', Meheryar said warming to the occasion, 'had a more realistic approach. He predicted that the state would cease to exist during the twentieth century if the standard was not found in fifty days — and so it did on the signing of the Treaty of Accession in 1950'.

Silence followed.

'There's more', Meheryar said, 'why not tell them his second prediction, Mama. I don't want them to link their future recollections of the prediction with me', Meheryar said.

'Well, I suppose they must be told,' Rani Satrangi said in well modulated tones, 'because it is part of Umrani history, which they should know'.

There was a pause before she spoke again.

'This man claimed that if the standard did not resurface within the first quarter of the twenty-first century, all the Umranis would perish by the end of 2130 and the family name would cease to exist'.

There was a gasp, then more silence. The younger Umranis shifted uneasily and avoided exchanging glances with anyone.

'Tell us about the third man,' Abby said shrilly to break the silence.

'You are a glutton for punishment', Bisma remarked. 'It gets worse.'

'No, she's entitled to know if she wants', Rani Satrangi said.

'Well, he was a strange bod. He turned up from the desert with a topknot, wearing a loin cloth, hairy and thickly bearded', Meheryar said. 'His body was covered with strange markings. He chanted Vedic verses which people thought strange and performed weird rites sitting cross legged in public places'.

'He was a sadhu', Rani Satrangi explained.

'Those who could make sense of his utterances described them as curses aimed at the rulers. Also invocations to his gods to inflict scourges and worse horrors on the populace'. Meheryar paused noting the effect of his remarks on his listeners.

Rani Satrangi took up the narration.

'They say that wherever the sadhu went, babies died or were stillborn, cattle and livestock perished, terrible accidents befell people and patches of blood appeared on land and water mysteriously. Things became so bad that people finally cornered him and stoned him to death. The body was never found. It seemed to have vanished. Instead the image of a bloodied skeleton would appear on moonless nights — still does, some claim. The British administration, caught unaware, hushed up the matter.'

A brooding silence followed. The spell was broken when Bisma's husband, Anwar Pasha walked in.

'What's happened?' he asked looking around. 'Such deep silence, such troubled faces. What's the matter?'

No one responded. Lunch was announced. Rani Satrangi got up and led them to the dining room.

# Chapter 6

Deriabad House in the port city came alive when three Deriabad State cars – followed by pickups and vans – swept in bearing a royal consignment. It included the Dowager Begum, Lady Ninette Umrani, her terriers, two princesses, household staff, tropical birds in custom built cages and other baggage associated with royalty. Drooping trees and petrified verdure lining the drive stirred and swayed. Silent lawns pricked up.

Deriabad House had a Bauhaus façade suggesting functional modernism which was somewhat at odds with the countrified setting of rambling gardens and flowering shrubs, but the combination seemed to have worked. It was the centerpiece of a farm on the outskirts of the port city. A seasonal riverbed – flooded during the monsoons – ran on the north-west of the farm.

Within a month of the move, Ninette hosted a reception for the glitterati. The princesses met some promising young persons that evening. Their social life took off.

Unknown to Ninette, her maid sent a weekly report of developments to Badshah Begum. Information of visits by callers on the princesses was a prominent aspect of the reports.

'What is Lady N up to?' Sartaj wondered, 'exposing the girls to the fast ways of the city.'

'That's because she is ignorant about our culture … and not the real mother of the girls,' Kulsoom said sneeringly.

'Don't jump to conclusions,' Badshah Begum interceded. 'Prospective suitors calling on the princesses is okay provided they are suitably matched in background and culture.'

'Proposals for Ala Hazrat's daughters should be forwarded to me at the palace, not to anyone else,' Sartaj said burping aloud. 'After all they are princesses and I, the Nawab of Deriabad.'

'Pomposity won't get you anywhere,' Badshah Begum said.

'So you see no harm if they go out to meet suitors,' Kulsoom persisted, 'unlike Bisma who received proposals while she lived in purdah at the palace.'

'That was the norm then ... Ala Hazrat was alive at the time, and the palace was his base. Things are different now. To start with there is no state ... and Sartaj is not a sovereign.'

'He is still head of a princely family.'

'Nowadays princes too have to adapt to the latest trends in courtship to prevent their marriageable daughters from becoming shelf cases.'

Ninette knew that the advent of her girls had brought a breath of fresh air to the social scene.

*They'll not want for suitors for long,* she concluded.

Her prediction came true. A succession of young men found their way to Deriabad House with flowers, chocolates and beating hearts. The princesses flitted gracefully between them enjoying the attention.

A major rift between Meheryar and Sartaj developed on account of Sartaj's churlished attitude towards Ninette and the girls. In one of his compulsive moments Sartaj reneged on his commitment to pay for the running of Deriabad House. The subsidy was resumed only after Meheryar stormed into his office, with clenched fists to remind him that Lady Ninette and the princesses were entitled 'as members of Ala Hazrat's family to household and maintenance expenses commensurate with their lifestyle and standard of living.' There was also a lurking fear that if he did not comply, Meheryar would make a reference to the ministry for resolution of Ninette's claim.

'Since, when have you become a champion of Lady N?' Sartaj asked sneeringly.

Meheryar hesitated, then smiled and said, 'Since our father married her and brought her into the family. The only family life he ever experienced was with Lady N and the girls ... you may have forgotten how it was ...'

A few months after the move to Deriabad House, Sadie surprised Ninette by announcing that she had received a proposal for marriage from a young man called Hussain Aminuddin, which she was inclined to accept.

Hussain had become a regular caller at Deriabad House after having met the girls at a party. It soon became clear that he was interested in Sadie. Hussain's family was prominent in business and social circles. It was also related to the Aga Khan, as a result of which it was usually linked with the Ismaili community, which regarded the Aga Khan as a spiritual leader.

Ninette wondered what Sartaj's reacton to the proposal would be. The matter assumed a formal aura when Hussain's parents called on Ninette at Deriabad House to make the proposal. She advised them to communicate the proposition to the ruler.

Her letter to Sartaj was written with a view to lay the ground diplomatically for the impending proposal. The Aminuddins sent a formally worded proposal to Sartaj. By coincidence both letters arrived at the same time. The formal proposal landed on his table like an ill-timed missile.

'What do these people think of themselves?' he yelled jumping up. 'They may be kings of industry but how dare they assume that they are good enough to marry into Ala Hazrat's family.'

He was about to fire off a letter rejecting the marriage proposal out of hand, but held back on seeing Ninette's letter. She had highlighted the positive aspects of the match: the international implications of the Aminuddin's kinship with the Aga Khan; Hussain's unquestioned eligibility;their prosperous lifestyle; their homes in London, Paris, New York and elsewhere. The ultimate trump card was Sadie's fondness for Hussain.

Unsettled by Ninette's reasoning, he took the matter home to Begum Badshah and meddlesome Kulsoom. Ninette had written earlier about Sadie to Badshah Begum. So she was not unprepared when Sartaj strode into her room at Moti Mahal to announce his rejection of the proposal.

'Intolerable,' he said, agitated and fidgeting.

'What is?' Badshah Begum asked.

'This proposal of marriage, sent by Mr. Aminuddin of the Ameen Tareen conglomerate.'

'Marriage with whom?' Kulsoom asked, her antenna alert.

'A proposal for Sadia for his son Hussain.'

'What nonsense,' Kulsoom cried out, 'how can an Aga Khani merchant presume to marry an Umrani princess.' A stream of red spittle found its way from her mouth to a *paan* spittoon.

'That's what I say,' Sartaj affirmed.

'Rejecting this marriage proposal from Mr. Aminuddin, who is President of the Ameen Tareen Bank, on grounds of social inferiority will make you look bad,' Badshah Begum said.

'I have stronger grounds for refusal,' Sartaj said. 'These people are not genuine Muslims.'

'What are you talking about?'

'They are Aga Khani Khojas or Ismaili Shi'as or some such sect who regard their leader as a Hazir imam … that's blasphemy. I can get a fatwa against them.'

'It is a *gunah* for us to marry them … worst kind of sin,' Kulsoom added.

'You're overreacting,' Badshah Begum said.

'What do you want me to do?' Sartaj asked irritably, 'Accept their proposal?'

'I didn't say anything of the kind, but I would advise you not to give such prejudiced reasons for non-acceptance. Too personal and highly impolitic. You should simply refuse without giving reason to avoid creating ill will. Use very polite language when doing so, like your father would have done.'

Sartaj paced up and down, muttering and shaking his head.

'How can Lady N have let things go so far?' He remarked.

'She should have known better.'

'She is not a Muslim,' Kulsoom said.

'Stop this kind of talk,' Badshah Begum snapped.

Sartaj continued pacing the room. Kulsoom took to filing her nails. Badshah Begum wondered what the ruler would have done in the circumstances.

Sartaj stopped for a moment at a window which framed a view of Lake Umrani and the spillover of the dam.

'I have asked for the opinion of ulema on the religious status of the Aminuddins,' he said. 'If they are found to be non-Muslims or apostates, I'll reject the proposal not by referring to their religious unsuitability, but on the grounds that the period of mourning following Ala Hazrat's death is not over.' He looked at the ladies expecting approval of the ruse he had suggested using.

'That's a feeble excuse,' Badshah Begum said. 'It doesn't even sound true … stop this ulema business … do as I say … write a polite letter expressing regrets on turning down the proposal … that's all … you are not obliged to give any reason.'

'I'll think about it,' Sartaj said starting for his office.

'Before writing to Mr. Aminuddin, write first to Lady N about your decision. It would be courteous and would also give you a chance to show concern for Sadia.'

'You mean adopt the gracious approach, Amma Huzoor.'

'I mean an approach befitting a ruler who is also head of a family.'

Ninette had an inkling about Sartaj's reaction, but when the expected happened, she was so disgusted by the reasons he gave that she was overcome by nausea.

*Twisted, warped idiot,* she mused. *Comme tragique, that someone as wise and noble as Shahryar should have such a successor.*

She dreaded telling Sadie about Sartaj's letter, but had to do so finally. The news of the refusal was a shock for Sadie. Stunned disbelief gave way to anger as the significance of Sartaj's views sank in.

'How can he say such awful things?' she raged. 'What right does she have to judge who is a Muslim and who not?'

A shaking fit seized Sadie causing her to slump into a chair. Ninette moved swiftly to calm her. Sadie broke into tears.

'I wish Daddy were alive,' she sobbed. 'He would have supported me. Instead we are landed with dreadful Sartaj Bhaijan. How are we going to deal with Hussain's family?'

'You care for him greatly?' Ninette enquired.

'More than anything else,' Sadie wailed.

'Then be patient … we're going to Deriabad, you and I … to have it out with that brother of yours. If you want Hussain, fight for him … and I'll fight with you.'

'What if he has written to them?'

'He's waiting for my comments, before he writes to them. He says so in the letter.'

Ninette put into effect an unusual strategy. She forwarded copies of her version of the situation accompanied by replications of Sartaj's letter to concerned family members. She notified them of her intention to visit Deriabad during the coming weekend for discussing issues related to the proposal at a family council she wanted convened. She requested them to attend the meeting for finding a solution to the problem.

Ninette and Sadie were relieved to see that Meheryar was at Deriabad airport to receive them.

The family council was held at the palace after a lunch attended by all those who were participating.

Sartaj sat at one end of the table, Badshah Begum at the other. Places in between were occupied by the two begums: Rani Satrangi, and Ninette, two princes: Meheryar and Behr-e-Karam, one consort: Kulsoom and Sadie.

Ninette started the discussion by thanking those present for attending at her call. The talks got slowly underway when she referred to certain portions of her written account. She responded in considerable detail to the queries raised by various family members. Sadie sat quietly throughout the talks. Sartaj also held his peace in the early part.

Kulsoom used the occasion to voice her concerns about the unwarranted freedom given to the princesses by exposing them to the liberal ways of port city society including unrestricted fraternisation between opposite sexes. Ninette firmly put down any suggestion of impropriety or excessiveness. She claimed that she took her maternal responsibilities as seriously as other Umrani mothers did. She pointed out that the confinement of the princesses to the Deriabad palace had kept them away from opportunities to meet desirable young people, make friends and come upon likely suitors. Life in the port city she pointed out, had changed the quality of their existence and put their lives in the right direction. They could now see some future prospects themselves, which was the appropriate outlook for persons their age to have.

'Sadie's interest in Hussain is a natural consequence of this approach,' she said. 'The question now is whether or not Hussain is suitable as a husband for Sadie.'

'My objection to him,' Sartaj said finally, 'is not based on social acceptability ... his blood ties with the Aga Khan are rated highly by some people ...'

'They were good enough for the British,' Meheryar said.

'Perhaps,' Sartaj replied, 'but from our standpoint they are traders ...'

'You were not going to make such remarks,' Badshah Begum cautioned.

'His trader status has nothing to do with my decision. I am concerned about Hussain's Ismaili connection. He is a Khoja and a Shi'a. Even if the Shi'a factor is overlooked, his Khoja status makes him a non-Muslim or an apostate.'

'On what do you base such assumptions, Bhaijan?' Meheryar asked.

'I sought the views of Moulvi Sahib.'

'Kulsoom's father,' Badshah Begum said deprecatingly.

'Not just him. His views are supported by some other ulema,' Sartaj said.

There was a pause.

'How do you see all this Lady Ninette?' Rani Satrangi asked trying to draw Ninette into the discussion.

'Whatever his belief, Sartaj's views are no more than a presumption,' Ninette remarked.

'Please elaborate,' Rani Satrangi said.

'Hussain's Muslim faith seems clear enough to me. He claims that by an affidavit filed with the registrar of the Bombay Presidency – during the days of British rule, and published simultaneously in the British Indian press – his great grandfather declared that as in the case of the Aga Khan, his family members were neither Nizari Ismaili nor Khoja.'

'Wasn't there a move to adhere only to the Prophet's faith instead of the Sunni Shi'a credos?' Meheryar asked.

'Yes, there was. Hussain's great grandfather declared *that* in a letter to the Aga Khan ... this was apparently followed by a purification prayer in the principal city mosque.'

'I suppose documentation of these matters is available,' Beher-e-Karam said.

'Yes,' Ninette said, 'I have some of it with me.'

'Then what's the problem?' Meheryar asked.

'He's still not a Muslim,' Kulsoom blurted out.

Sartaj glared at her for interrupting.

'Hold your tongue,' Badshah Begum said.

'I don't understand,' Rani Satrangi said shaking her head.

'The ulema are of the view that these declarations were not correct procedure,' Sartaj said in response to Rani Satrangi. 'They claim to be neither Shi'a nor Sunni ... simply Muslims as they put it ... a sort of tailor-made Islam to suit their needs, which is not acceptable to purists.'

'No need to belittle them,' Badshah Begum said.

'I don't see how Hussain's claim is deniable,' Ninette said, 'He prays five times, studies the Quran with meaning, is learning Arabic, observes the prescribed duties, has been on Haj twice, supports several charities including a madrasa for boys and one for girls ... if he is not a Muslim, I wonder who is?'

'I am sorry Lady Ninette,' Sartaj said, 'I am bound by the ulema's opinion.'

Sadie was about to get up and speak. Ninette held her back, and spoke in her stead, 'Such an extreme step Sartaj is not going to stop your sister from marrying Hussain ... that is what I believe Sadie was about to say.'

There was palpable silence.

'You mean, she will get married even if the head of the family forbids it?' Kulsoom asked.

'You heard me,' Ninette said. 'She expected – as most of us did – a decision worthy of a head of family, something her father would have given ... not a bigoted ... or doctrinaire ruling.'

The veins stood out on Sartaj temples.

'If she does get married without approval,' Sartaj said raising his voice, 'then she'll no longer be treated as a member of this family. I'll write to the states ministry to strip her of her title.'

This was an outcome no one foresaw. A stunned silence filled the room. After a while, Rani Satrangi spoke in well modulated tones, 'Sadia can get married in Do Minar Haveli ... I will be happy to co-host the wedding with her mother, Lady Ninette.'

Meheryar went across and kissed his mother,

'Bravo Mama ... I want everyone to know that my residence will also be available to my sister.'

Behr-e-Karam was the next one to speak,

'No question about it, Sadie also has my home to choose from.'

'This much is clear then, that those of us who have spoken will participate in her wedding,' Meheryar said. 'Our little sister will be sent off in accordance with her birthright from Deriabad.'

Sartaj got up abruptly and walked away from the proceedings. Caught off guard, Kulsoom hoisted her bulk and padded after him. Badshah Begum looked distinctly uncomfortable. As far as she was concerned, things had ended badly – Sartaj had come off poorly in the encounter. His intransigence had created a rift in the family.

Ninette dried her tears. Sadie hugged her and all others present. When parting Ninette thanked them.

'We feel very strong now with your backing,' she said. 'Nice having a family that cares.'

A few days after their return to the port city, Ninette received a package from Badshah Begum. In the accompanying letter she mentioned her regret at the way in which the council meeting ended. Sartaj's stand, she explained was based on his belief of it being the right decision. Irrespective of whether it was correct or erroneous, she expressed unstinted support for Sadie's marriage. She could not have done so at the meeting without embarrassing Sartaj. She offered to help with the wedding expenses. Two sets of her own trousseau jewellry were enclosed as her contribution to Sadie's trousseau.

With Badshah Begum's announcement supporting the marriage, the last post had fallen. Sartaj's offer to host his sister's wedding followed a few days later. It was to be the first family wedding at Falaktaj Palace after the ruler's death.

# Chapter 7

Javed Rizvi was elated when the Chief Secretary, States and Frontier Regions directed him to travel to Deriabad to discuss certain matters with Prince Behr-e-Karam. Such a task would normally have been assigned to an official of the rank of a deputy secretary but the secretary had chosen to depute him instead.

The first setback to this windfall came in the guise of the travel and accommodation allowances for the task. Under departmental rules, they were restricted to paltry sums for section officers. The travel budget was barely sufficient for a train or coach trip to Deriabad. Both alternatives entailed a journey of ten hours. The living allowance was confined to two star accommodations.

In Deriabad he would be meeting Major Tariq, representing the GHQ interest in the discussions. The more generous terms of the GHQ had enabled Major Tariq to take a flight to Deriabad and stay in the five star comfort of a palace converted into Shahpasand Hotel. He met Javed Rizvi expansively in the lobby which offered a fine view of the Deriabad hills surrounding Lake Umrani. They were expecting Behr-e-Karam to join them for lunch in a private dining room.

Behr-e-Karam looked older than twenty-seven. He was lean, well turned out and noticeable in a crowd not only for his resemblance to the ruler but also for his cavalier style that marked him out from the rest.

'When I got your email,' he said addressing Major Tariq, 'I was somewhat puzzled … but the detailed letter from the Ministry of States and Frontier Regions made the situation clearer.'

'Glad to hear that,' Javed Rizvi put in between mouthfuls of grilled fish

'From what I understand, you chaps want me to be your look- out in Deriabad.'

'Something like that,' Major Tariq said, shifting in his chair.

'But why?'

'We need to know what's going on.'

'What could be going on in this ... this backwater?'

'Quite a lot Prince,' Major Tariq said, in response to Behr-e-Karam's raised eyebrow, 'a new ruler not quite firmly installed, the growing popularity of Prince Meheryar who the local feudal lobby would prefer as nawab, the two hundred kilometer boundary in the Satrang desert shared with our contentious neighbouring country, strategic building works taking place across the border, the ground roots movement for Deriabad to break away into an autonomous federal unit, Princess Bisma Sultan's bid to stand as an independent candidate in the election, Prince Sartaj's support for the King's party by endorsing the National Front candidates.'

Behr-e-Karam smiled taking in the Major's comments.

'But Major,' he said finally, 'Why would you want me to spy on my own family? You have listening posts all over the country who keep you up to date on developments...'

'They are ... street level operators. We want a person who is within the hierarchy.'

'I see. Why haven't you approached Prince Meheryar?'

Major Tariq and Javed Rizvi exchanged glances.

'He is an interested party, closely linked with some of our concerns,' Javed Rivi said hastily, to assert his place in the discussion.

'Also Prince, from what we know of him,' Major Tariq said, 'he is unlikely to cooperate in this regard.'

'You're right. Deriabad interests are his topmost priority. He won't compromise them in any way,' Behr-e-Karm said.

'What do you expect me to do? I'm not about to prepare detailed reports for you.'

'Nothing like that Prince. With your permission, I will call or email you with specific queries, and would appreciate your oral or email responses. It will be me largely who will communicate with you, but Mr. Rizvi may have some enquiries from the ministry. Other than that, if anything at all concerning these or other matters strikes you as significant, please advise us by email or cell phone as convenient.'

'I take it that all this will be confidential,' Behr-e-Karam said. 'I would not like anyone, family member or other person except for your superiors dealing with these matters – to know of my involvement.'

'Rest assured, Prince. We would not succeed in such matters if we disclosed our sources. In return for your cooperation, you will have the gratitude of your government and recourse to its good offices for obtaining passport, visas, foreign exchange and other matters within its purview, along with a substantial honorarium the details of which I will disclose to you in due course.'

'I'll call and let you know by the end of the week, if I agree to your proposal.'

Behr-e-Karam walked away knowing that he would accept the offer. It was one way for him to stay in the picture. It would also help in creating a favourable image of him in official circles.

Bisma smiled when she learnt that the standard had been assigned to her as an election symbol. She was at a meeting in her office attended by her work team. Her campaign manager, Ghulam Ali, was busy explaining the countrywide distribution of the Federal Assembly seats. He went on to mention that Deriabad had fifteen seats in the Federal Assembly.

'That works out to five for each of the three districts into which Deriabad is subdivided,' he confirmed.

'You must stand from a constituency in each district ... not just Satrangbela,' Almas, a hijab wearing worker, said excitedly.

'Is that what you advise?' Bisma asked glancing at the assembled campaigners.

'Yes Princess, most of us feel you should be contesting in all three districts of Deriabad,' Ghulam Ali said.

'Is that really your considered opinion?'

Many voices responded positively.

'You will be making a statement for us,' Almas said. 'It should be heard all over.'

'In that case we'll need to go back to the election commission to sign up for two more constituencies,' Bisma said.

'That won't be a problem,' Ghulam Ali said. 'We could go tomorrow.'

'We will have to start canvassing in all three constituencies.' Almas said.

'Of course,' Ghulam Ali said, 'but that means separate teams for covering the different constituencies,'

The office of the Tehreek-e-Awam in Deriabad was based in a shop next to the central mosque. It had initially been a retail outlet for prayer caps, rosaries, prayer mats, attar and other devotional bric a brac. When the owner was appointed as zonal representative of the Tehreek and asked to find centrally located premises for the party office, he terminated the business and rented the space to the party.

In the office, Ameer Bakhsh – by now fully committed to follow retired Air Vice Marshal Changez Khan Turkmanzai, nicknamed *Sona munda* (handsome lad), founder of the Tehreek-e-Awam – was occupied with one of the computers when a Deriabad Mercedes approached the roundabout on its way to the election commission. He observed a veiled lady alight from the car and proceed to the commission office accompanied by Ghulam Ali and a hijab clad woman.

His curiosity was allayed at the mosque when a clerk of the election commission informed him between prayers that Princess Bisma Sultan would now be contesting the election from three Deriabad constituencies, FA 148, FA 150 and FA 153.

The sun was setting by the time Ameer Bakhsh got to Pattanwala. His homecoming was usually an uplifting moment for the family. After greeting his mother, and father – if the latter was home at the time – he would catch up with the children and his siblings before bathing and settling down.

This time he failed to connect with the family. Instead, he bathed, prayed and retreated to the roof. When Razia went up with his tea, she heard him mutter, 'If she can do it so can I.'

'If who can do what?' she asked.

'Nothing,' he said, looking up startled.

'Tell me,' Razia said. 'You don't talk to me these days … you don't even have time for the children … always angry … always moody … everything seems to have changed since you decided to stand for elections.' She stood behind him massaging his shoulders.

'No change really. I have things on my mind.'

'Your mother finds you changed. The children too. You don't come to me any more. Before we were together every few days. Its been weeks since you touched me.'

'Stop this kind of talk Razia. I told you certain matters need to be resolved first.'

'At least tell me what you were talking to yourself about.'

'It's the election. I am planning, to stand from three separate constituencies.'

'Why? Isn't one enough?'

'My party wants me to win. My chances of winning are better if I contest three constituencies.'

'Who are the contestants against you, nawab saheb's people?'

'No. They're there but they are not my main rivals.'

'Who then?'

'Shahzadi Bisma Sultan.'

'Ya Allah! How can you even think of contesting the election against her.'

'I have as good a chance as she does.'

'Why do you want to do this? They are nawabs and we, peasants. They have their way, we ours. Why should we try to enter their space?'

'You're an ignorant woman. An election is open for anyone to contest – no nawabs, no peasants. Everyone has an equal chance. This is my moment to go ahead, to serve the country if I am successful – *Insha'Allah.*'

'Ignorant woman I may be but I know my place.' For a moment Ameer Bakhsh felt like she did. She looked so winsome and vulnerable, yet grounded in reality. Then he turned away.

# Chapter 8

Allah Bakhsh approached every grave at the Umrani tomb site, recited a prayer for the deceased, lighted an incense stick and strewed a handful of rose petals and marigolds. The custodian came upon him as he was wielding a duster on the graves in the mausoleum of the nawabs. They embraced and shook hands.

'Is it time already for your annual visit?' he asked Allah Bakhsh.

'Not exactly,' Allah Bakhsh replied, 'I was close by checking on a report about squatters on Umrani lands, so I decided to come here to pay respects.'

'Is all well my brother?'the custodian asked showing concern.

'All's well, and not well. The older boy Ameer Bakhsh has taken up politics. He is contesting the elections.'

'Federal or provincial?'

'Federal … God help him. The second one has left for Dubai … doesn't want to work for the Umranis. The third boy wants to become a computer technologist after he leaves college. Both the unmarried girls want to continue with their education, hoping to specialise in some fields, and take up jobs.'

'Winds of change,' the custodian said, 'that's the new generation. No one wants to do what their parents did. Not good enough for them. They want to go off and do something better.'

Echoes of the conversation were picked up deep underground by Canny Kamran.

'They're learning time tested truths ... nothing remains the same ... least of all descendants, they ring the changes ... precursors of new ages.'

'More graveyard wisdom Canny,' Fussy Farhad remarked.

'What was that remark about an election?' Soofi Saeen asked.

'Who cares,' Grumbles muttered.

'There's a rumour that Bisma, Steadfast Shahryar's daughter is standing for election,' Curioso said.

'*La houl walah!*' Greybeard, remarked, 'What next ... when princes adopt the practices of peasants, beggars ascend thrones.'

'Stop mixing metaphors,' the Eldest Elder commented, 'and let Steadfast Shahryar be ... he must complete his slumber before he is fully conditioned to join us.'

The sound of a motorcycle disturbed the silence of the graveyard. As it neared the tomb site Allah Bakhsh stopped sipping tea and sat up.

'What is it?' the custodian asked putting down his mug.

'I think it's Ameer Bakhsh come to fetch me.'

'But you came by bus.'

'The return journey by bus is not due for another two and a half hours. Since Ameer Bakhsh was in the area electioneering, I asked him to pick me up.'

By the time Allah Bakhsh finished speaking, the motorcycle's drone had passed by the graveyard, moving onwards in the opposite direction, and receding into the distance.

Ameer Bakhsh was indeed in the area but at the time he was conducting a corner meeting in Mazarian Wali, a village serving as a bus terminus some distance from the graveyard.

'Of course we have a manifesto,' he declared hoarsely over a makeshift loud speaker, 'better than the manifestos put out by other parties, but I'm not here to convince you of the strength of our programme. I'm here to ask you to think about the strengths of the leader of the Tehreek-e-Awam party, retired Air Vice Marshal Changez Khan Turkmanzai – strengths the whole country has been hearing and reading about on the national media for the last three years – strengths that give rise to

44

legends and then make up your mind which one of the leaders in the field today will deliver what he has promised.' He paused to gauge the effect of his words on the hundred odd yokels present.

'A manifesto simply states a party's political objectives. It is no more than a collection of ideas. It is unable to get anything done on its own but a leader can get things done. It is the leader who gives life to the manifesto ...'

'We have seen many of these leaders,' called out a young man in a lungi with a Palestinian keffiyeh slung over his shoulders. 'What difference have they brought to our lives? We continue to labour in poverty like our fathers and grandfathers did and which our grandsons will have to face. We have never got anything from these leaders.'

A murmur rose. Ameer Bakhsh felt he was being upstaged by the remarks from the crowd.

'I don't claim that Changez Khan will give you the better life which you deserve. No one other than Allah can change things overnight, but if one leader in a million commits himself to a programme that gives power to the people, there will be change for the better, and if the programme continues without interruption for five to ten years, the change will start affecting the lives of citizens. That is the only way a country can improve. That is the way countries like China, Malaysia, Singapore and Indonesia have improved.'

'You talk of a leader – a man – improving the country, when many such have ruined the country,' a boy, barely seventeen, sporting a wispy beard, spoke. 'Why not rely on parties with strong moral programmes, like the Jamaat-e-Islami?'

'We are not like advanced countries,' Ameer Bakhsh responded, 'that have benefited from generations of good governance which has strengthened their institutions. I mean those institutions that are driven by ideology and not by individuals. To get to that stage we need many years of good governance. And that will come not from strong moral programmes, but from strong leadership having the guts to implement morally sound programmes.'

'If we do not like any leader, do we still have to vote?' asked an older peasant squatting on his haunches.

'If people did not vote, no one would be elected and there would be no change in the country. The only way you can bring about change,' Ameer Bakhsh said pointing a forefinger at the peasant, 'is by voting. Your votes will bring in a leader. If he is a good leader, he will work for you benefit.'

In a teashop close to the site of the corner meeting, the overseer of the largest landowner of the area nursed his mug of tea and called his boss by cell phone.

'What is it boy?' came in the rasping tones of Malik Azad Khan.

'Salam ailekum *saeen*,' the overseer replied, 'I am at a teashop in Mazarian Wali. Ameer Bakhsh son of Allah Bakhsh Lashari, head *baildar* of nawab *saeen's* family is holding a corner meeting for *Sona munda's* party.'

'How is it that nawab *saeen's* man is supporting *Sona munda?*'

'This chap does not have the same political loyalties as his father.'

'How is the meeting going?'

'Can't tell, It's been on for an hour and no one is leaving.'

'Well you know what to do. That fellow has no right to campaign for our opponent in our area. Drive him out.'

The overseer rounded up thirty or so of his tenants, handed them National Front banners and led them to the meeting site, sloganeering loud enough to drown out the voices at the corner meeting. The unexpected appearance of the NF group caught Ameer Bakhsh by surprise. He turned up the volume on the loud speaker and pitched a higher tone. His workers jumped into the fray by shouting back at the hecklers. The resulting cacophony drowned out all other noises.

Matters became worse when the hecklers, egged on by the overseer, began to pelt Ameer Bakhsh's men with pebbles. Some of the pebbles went awry hitting spectators at the site. Within minutes the opposing sides, and the injured spectators were pelting each other with missiles gravitating from pebbles to stones. Several more tenants kept coming from somewhere to reinforce the overseer's team.

When the supply of missiles became scarce, fist fights and grappling broke out. Shopkeepers fearing for the safety of their premises dispatched emissaries on motorcycles to the nearest police station on a SOS mission.

The number of the wounded kept increasing causing tempers to rise. As the conflict escalated, wooden staffs and staves were brandished and wielded. A sudden burst of gunfire halted the fighting momentarily before it was resumed with greater intensity. At the sound of police sirens most of the combatants scattered. Some slunk away to avoid the police. Others moved to a side passing themselves off as bystanders.

A dozen policemen spilled out of transport vehicles and baton charged those who continued fighting. They were taken into custody and bundled into the vehicles for enquiry at the police station. Many others were rounded up for on scene questioning and site investigation.

The overseer and his henchmen were not to be seen. Ameer Bakhsh's workers found him lying face down under two unconscious bodies. He had been beaten severely with hard objects. His body was a mass of bruises, bleeding wounds and broken bones.

On learning about the police raid, Malik Azad Khan put calls through to local officials responsible for law and order, seeking exoneration for himself from any involvement in the fracas. He wanted the police report to implicate Ameer Bakhsh's team as troublemakers and inciters of violence who were responsible for launching the attack on his men. His contacts advised him to discuss these matters directly with the SHO at the police station.

'Despite any instructions we give him to say what you want, he will prepare the FIR in his own terms so you should approach him first,' they emphasised. 'Since the press has already publicised the incident as the first pre-election breach of law and order, he will be keen to dispel any charge of police bungling.'

Malik Azad was seen later that evening calling on the SHO at the station, with a roll of newspapers in hand. When he left the SHO's office forty-five minutes later the newspaper roll was not with him.

The FIR issued the following day found Ameer Bakhsh and his workers responsible for attacking the NF procession. Charges filed in due course resulted in the institution of criminal proceedings which would necessitate Ameer Bakhsh's presence periodically at the Deriabad sessions court for the next several months.

The children from Allah Bakhsh's homestead were the first to reach the pick-up that bore the injured from Mazarian Wali to Pattanwala. On seeing the bandaged bodies, bloodied and swollen they ran wildly indoors calling out to their elders.

Razia rushed out followed by her ten year old daughter and seven year old son. Her snot nosed three year old stood half naked at the doorstep, howling at being abandoned. On seeing Ameer Bakhsh's crumpled body, Razia fainted. Ameer Bakhsh's mother, Masuda Mai screamed loudest and beat her breast. Ameer Bakhsh's sisters held on to her and drew her back to the home. Soon women from neighbouring homes gathered, some wailing and protesting about injuries suffered by party workers to whom they were related. Others came offering comfort and support.

Ameer Bakhsh and Razia were borne indoors by his brothers. When Allah Baksh returned, it was to a house in clamour. He had learnt about the Mazarian Wali incident earlier that day, so he dreaded the scene at home. It took him a while to restore calm.

'No one is dead,' he yelled at the wailing women. 'Ameer Bakhsh's wounds will heal. The doctors who attended to him say that he will recover fully from this terrible experience.'

Ameer Bakhsh had sustained many injuries – fractures of the left tibia, ribcage and three fingers, sprained neck, multiple cuts and bruises and loss of faith in the sanctity of straight forward electioneering.

Masuda Mai's stolidity that usually kept the family going during crises, seemed to have deserted her. Her hysterical outbursts at her son's battered condition kept everyone in sobbing fits. It was left to the stiff lipped Allah Bakhsh to take control and restore a sense of normality.

Ameer Bakhsh was feverish and delirious for two nights. Masuda Mai tended to him personally, pushing Razia aside when she attempted to reach Ameer Bakhsh. She would give up her cot side vigil only to a doctor or compounder. To escape her angry reproaches, her grandchildren kept to the rooftop.

On the third day, Ameer Bakhsh opened his eyes to find his father at his bedside. His mother slept seated on a stool, her head on the cot. Allah Baksh murmured a prayer then touched Ameer Bakhsh's forehead with his lips.

'I'm sorry Abbaji,' Ameer Bakhsh whispered.

'Nothing to be sorry for son … you were doing what you believed in and for that you were attacked …' his voice caught in a sob.

'More trouble for you …' Ameer Bakhsh started to say but stopped when he looked at his father's eyes. Not dismay but admiration was what he saw.

Meheryar came to Pattanwala village to see Ameer Bakhsh and to offer help to Allah Bakhsh. He urged the local law and order keepers to trace the Mazarian Wali hecklers and indict them but as officialdom had been instructed to favour the National Front, no indictment was likely. Sartaj and the other Umranis – at Sartaj's behest – maintained a distance from their *baildar's* family. Sartaj had no option but to toe the 'official' line.

An innate sense of survival speeded Ameer Bakhsh's recovery. The cuts and bruises vanished in a few days aided by a residual solidity and smouldering anger. Razia felt her husband had moved on. The children sensed it too. His announcement of reconvening the corner meeting that was interrupted was met with objections from Razia and his mother.

Allah Bakhsh put an end to the controversy by stating,'Your political stance is all wrong. You have chosen the wrong side, but I have faith in your faith … you have my blessings.'

His appearance with crutches some weeks later at the corner meeting in Mazarian Wali had the locals from the earlier meeting and others who came expecting more fisticuffs, clapping and cheering. There was no sign of the overseer or his thugs.

The police were present in abundance. They looked on resentfully as Ameer Bakhsh's performance that day won him the Mazarian Wali vote bank before even the ballot had been cast.

# Chapter 9

Minister in waiting Mehboob Alam Shah had been trying for a while to get through by telephone to the federal capital. He wanted to speak to Anwar Pasha who held the post of Deputy Secretary at the Ministry of Defence. When at last someone at the ministry picked up the receiver, he was informed that Anwar Pasha had left by car for Deriabad.

*So he's coming home,* Mehboob Alam Shah realised, *he might at least have told me before setting out …maybe he has the information I want.*

Mehboob Alam Shah turned to his cell phone to call Anwar Pasha. Minutes later he got a response.

'Is that you, Shahji?'

'Yes sir, been trying you at your office.'

'I'm on my way to Deriabad. You'll see me sooner than expected … anyway what are you calling about?'

'Have States and Frontier Regions slashed the privy purse?'

'Rumour has it that that has been done. Why? Did you expect otherwise?'

'Not quite … I am aware of the Treaty terms but the responsibility for certain expenditure outlays has not been resolved. Take the public utility requirements of palace establishments and the cantonment. These were serviced by civic agencies we set up, the costs of which were met from privy purse establishment allocations. The agencies are not under our control now. They have been taken over by the local government which, as you are aware, is subject to the provincial government. Are we expected to continue bearing their expenses under the new arrangement?'

'I don't know these details, Shahji. You'd be better advised to approach the S&FR ministry, but knowing the federal government's policy of slashing outgoings to subordinate bodies and funnelling the slashed sums to the pockets of its incumbents ...' the line dropped terminating further conversation.

*If the bastards do that, we're finished ... Dumbo will have a fit ... well, at least it will pull him down a peg or two from the high he's been on since he became nawab,* went through Mehboob Alam Shah's mind.

Bisma and Anwar Pasha's home was on a hillside with a view of Deriabad. It had the look of a Mediterranean villa. Bisma Sultan ran an office in an outhouse for her election campaign. She watched her husband's car – now visible, now screened by trees – winding its way up the hill. He had informed her of his homecoming by cell phone two hours before arrival. Bisma carried on discussing the timetable of her election strategy with her workers.

Finding no one at the villa, other than the major-domo, Anwar Pasha set off for the outhouse, a frown creasing his forehead. He knocked. A well modulated voice – reminiscent of Rani Satrangi – responded in uncharacteristic crisp tones, 'Wait at the villa Anwar, I'll be there in fifteen minutes.'

They were married fourteen years earlier. It was a fairy tale wedding, if ever. Deriabad was transformed into a festival town. Flowers, bunting and freshly painted shop fronts enlivened the streets. At night the town shone like a luminous planet visible from afar. Banners in the seven rainbow shades displayed prayers for the couple, praise and affection for the nawab and family.

Musicians, dancing girls and street shows flocked to Deriabad. A carnival and a circus drew crowds in the evening. During the day visitors had access to the public rooms in the palaces, the museum, antiquity sites, the zoo, parks, water headworks, the Umrani dam and picnic sites.

All this to celebrate the wedding of a breathtakingly beautiful couple, with a love story to match.

Twelve years later the marriage existed in name only. There were no children. Although Bisma could have conceived, Anwar Pasha could not impregnate her. She had taken this in her stride, since he was not to blame. She loved him too much to let it come in the way, but she could not ignore the indignities suffered in time – alcoholism laced with violence, male and female lovers, embezzlement of palace funds, missing antiquities, loans that had to be settled by the nawab and Rani Satrangi, bribery and corruption in federal government assignments.

Anwar Pasha was not equal to Bisma in any way that mattered. She had inherited a fineness from her parents. To save face she had continued with the marriage, keeping her problems to herself. Despite her silence, Rani Satrangi's maternal instinct had discerned her daughter's woes. Female intuitiveness had also alerted Badshah Begum, Kulsoom and Ninette to the turmoil in Bisma's life. Her brothers too sensed that all was not as it should be in the lives of the golden couple, assuming that Bisma's interest in politics was motivated by the need for adding purpose to life. Anwar Pasha continued to love her, believing – mistakenly – that he could reform and win her love back despite the broken promises that littered the years of married life.

Anwar Pasha was pacing up and down the hallway when Bisma turned up. She offered a cheek perfunctorily to him and moved away before he could kiss her other cheek. Your visit is unexpected. What brings you to Deriabad?' she asked.

'I've come to talk to you,' he replied.

'To me, what about?'

'Bisma, the capital is buzzing with news of you taking part in the election.'

The major-domo – a leftover from her father's time – walked in stiff as a ramrod preceding a tea tray borne by a liveried butler.

'Shall we sit here,' she said indicating a niche with mock aplomb, 'with our tea-cups and discuss the capital's concern about my election plans.'

'The generals egged on by the mullah lobby are against your participation.'

'Even though I am standing from my home constituency?'

'Despite the support you'll get, they don't want a woman like you in the Assembly.'

'Is it me they object to or women in general?'

'Don't be childish Bisma ... you know how they think. They just don't want someone as high profile as you in the political pile.'

'Do they have nothing better to do than fret about the politics of a female from a non-existent state?'

'They believe that if you get in, whichever party has majority in the Assembly will seek your support in the block that it uses for confronting the army on contentious policy matters.'

'And so?'

'They fear that in such situations you are likely to side with those who will not toe the army line.'

'That is clever of them. It's a sound assessment of my likely approach in such situations.'

'They have pressured me to dissuade you from taking part in the election and hinted at the likelihood of negative policy decisions affecting Deriabad and also my career in government if I fail.'

Bisma pondered a while before replying, 'Anwar, you and I differ on many things, but you know me enough to realise that threats and sanctions have never deterred me from what I believe to be the right course of action.'

'Are you going to take the generals on?' Anwar Pasha asked alarmed.

'My decision to enter politics did not come lightly. It was – and is – against my normal inclinations to go public in this manner, but there is so much that is wrong with the part of the world we live in that the only effective means by which someone like me, who is not a general, a political mafiosa, a religious demagogue or revolutionary can do something about it is by joining the national game and playing for power stakes. There is no other way of becoming effective in affairs of state. It's a long shot, and may take forever but the alternative is to stand by and let bad things happen.'

She got up and made for the staircase. While ascending she said, 'If my decision creates waves for Sartaj Bhaijan or you, you'll have to fend for yourselves. I'll be far too occupied watching my back.'

'Bisma's decision is wrong, wrong, wrong,' Sartaj fumed.

'Imagine,' Kulsoom remarked, 'an Umrani princess in politics, going out in public seeking votes.'

'It's against the family policy of staying away from politics … it's also a breach of the purdah tradition of our ladies,' Behr-e-Karam said.

Sartaj had been briefed earlier by Anwar Pasha on the power brokers' stance on Bisma's candidature, and her response to their views. Sartaj had reacted by calling a meeting of family members whom he felt were likely to endorse his point of view. Badshah Begum, Behr-e-Karam and Anwar Pasha were present.

'Amma Huzoor,' Sartaj said, 'will you speak to Rani Satrangi Saheb and to Bisma Sultan on this matter?'

'No harm in speaking to them, but I don't see Bisma withdrawing from the election,' Badshah Begum said. 'She's far too committed,'

'Did she inform any of us about her decision … or seek advice before filing her papers?' Kulsoom enquired.

There was a pause.

'She did circulate a letter amongst all adult family members, disclosing her intention to join politics,' Behr-e-Karam said.

'But not that she was standing for election as an independent candidate,' Kulsoom added.

'It's a bit late to raise these issues now,' Badshah Begum said pointedly.

'But Amma Huzoor,' Sartaj said, 'what she does will affect all of us … there will some serious repercussions for Deriabad State interests.'

'I do think … when a family member acts in matters that affect the rest, some notice of his or her intentions should be given, especially to those whose interests are likely to be affected … and some form of consensus on the outcome should be reached, but in all my years in Deriabad I've not come across family members resolving problems by consensus,' Badshah Begum said.

'Father did not teach us that discipline,' Behr-e-Karam said. 'We were never encouraged to consult amongst ourselves or take account of others' views.'

'A leftover of the colonial policy of divide and rule …' Sartaj put in.

'Don't criticise Ala Hazrat,' Badshah Begum snapped. 'He was a single child who had no experience of dealing with brothers and sisters. When he was made nawab at the age of eight, he had no one to rely on. It was a feat for him, surviving in times when inconvenient rulers were done away with by poison, accident or exposure to infections.'

'He was indeed an exemplary ruler, if not an ideal father,' Behr-e-Karam added.

'Since Anwar Pasha has not be able to convince Bisma Sultan to give up the election,' Badshah Begum said, 'how can we hope to succeed?'

'We can try talking to her with all present … it may work if she sees enough of us have objections,' Beher-e-Karam said.

They did just that. At the end of the discussion, Bisma, who had listened attentively to their views, said, 'My dear family members, I have noted your concern. I think that even if I had sought consensus before making a move, I would have heard the views stated today. So I will say now what I would have said then: I'm taking this step not only for Deriabad but for the nation of which Deriabad is now a part.'

On hearing Bisma's response, Sartaj's anger was all too apparent. He accused her of indifference to Deriabad's welfare, disloyalty to the family, dishonouring the Umranis and placing self-interest foremost.

'So soon after father's death, you are destroying what he stood for,' He spat out, scowling. The others sat in shocked silence during the tirade.

'When it was over, Bisma said, 'I will remember all you have said Sartaj Bhaijan, and when the time is right I will come to you for reviewing the accuracy of each charge.'

To cover his tracks, Behr-e-Karam reported the matter to Meheryar.

'Enough is enough,' Meheryar fumed thumping his fist on a table when he learned of Sartaj's denouncement of Bisma.

'He is a petty man who uses his authority to tyrannize his family,' he told Rani Satrangi, 'I am going to sort him out once and for all.'

'Careful how you go about it. He is still head of the family and can harm you,'

'I can harm him more than he can me,' Meheryar said, grimly.

Sartaj turned pale when confronted by Meheryar in this mood. 'What gives you the right to deal with family members in the way you do?' Meheryar demanded.

'As the nawab,' Sartaj spluttered, 'I use my authority in the best interest of the family and the institution of Deriabad.'

'By cutting off the maintenance allowance for Deriabad House? By denying Sadie the right to marry someone who you call a non-Muslim? By accusing Bisma of disloyalty to the family for exercising her right to stand for election? These are mean, spiteful acts unworthy of a ruler. As for upholding the institution of state, I know of many instances where you have cut justifiable expenditure on the upkeep of palace properties … you exercise your authority only to punish and spite your family and personnel. I don't think you are fit to be nawab …' Meheryar said.

'What … what do you mean?' Sartaj mumbled shocked.

'I've coped with your pathetic fumbling and guided you due to my commitment to the institution of state and the Umrani family, but I am damned if I continue working with you in these circumstances. So I am resigning from the post of Chief Advisor.' Meheryar said placing his letter of resignation on Sartaj's table before walking out.

Panic struck, Sartaj rushed to Badshah Begum for advise.

'You were wrong to do those things … he is justified in that,' she said putting on her glasses, 'but we must try to rectify the situation. You'll be lost without him … you know that well enough … it's not just the administration, but dealing with the federal government … also our commercial projects are doing well because of him.'

Sartaj sat with his head in his hands, tears in his eyes, ruing his limitations.

After a while Badshah Begum said, 'You must write a letter asking him to stay on for the sake of the institution and undertake to be fair and sympathetic in dealing with family and palace staff, to seek his advice when faced with controversial matters … I will draft the letter for you.'

The letter went out the next day. Badshah Begum followed it up by calling on Rani Satrangi to enlist her support.

A week later Meheryar was back at his post.

# Chapter 10

Electioneering paraphernalia became more evident in Deriabad as summer heat melded into misty autumn. Posters advertising names, faces and parties of the candidates appeared all over. Slogans in graffiti were scrawled on bare walls. Faces of prominent members of political families were emblazoned on giant billboards – like the cast of a Lollywood epic movie – in support of their party candidates. Corner meetings were held and rallies thronged the streets.

Bisma's face was not displayed on account of her royal status and seemingly in compliance with the purdah tradition of the royal ladies. Instead, her posters bore her name along with a facsimile of the Umrani coat of arms and a representation of her election symbol, a standard in the form of a fluttering pennant.

Behr-e-Karam sat in on a meeting called by Sartaj at the palace for discussing election plans with the candidates nominated by the National Front for the Deriabad seats. His assiduous courting of Sartaj and Kulsoom after having entered into the trading of information deal with Major Tariq, had won him a place in Sartaj's inner circle.

The brothers sat at an oval table in an ante-chamber next to the Darbar Hall awaiting the candidates. They were ushered in by minister in waiting, Mehboob Alam Shah. They greeted Sartaj with great respect. His response was cool. Behr-e-Karam was more courteous.

There were fifteen candidates altogether for the Deriabad constituencies. Some were seasoned politicians, most of them were feudal or religio-feudal, all were election winners. They sat around the table while refreshments were served. Mehboob Alam flanked by a stenographer, video and sound recordists sat at adjoining tables.

Sartaj started the proceedings by questioning each candidate about his campaign programme. A detailed discussion on election strategy followed. Sartaj exhorted them to put up a grand presentation. Something the public had not seen before. He wanted lights, music, concerts and pop singers.

'You all have the means to afford such things' he pointed out. 'I believe the party has also allocated sufficient funds for the Deriabad seats … campaign jointly or individually as you please … both methods should work … anyhow you know best … some of you are past masters at the election game.'

'What guidance can you give us about our leading opponents, Your Highness?' a candidate enquired quietly.

Sartaj turned to Mehboob Alam making out as if he required briefing before replying.

'Your Highness,' Mehboob Alam mumbled, jumping up, 'there is Ameer Bakhsh Lashari standing on the Tehreek-e-Awam ticket and – and there's Maulana Anwarullah from the Jamaat-e-Muslimeen, and – and …'

'And there's our sister, Sahibzadi Bisma Sultan standing as an independent candidate,' Behr-e-Karam finished off.

Sartaj grimaced at the mention of Bisma's name.

'Quite an impressive array,' remarked a candidate.

'The Tehrik-e-Awam,' said another, 'has gained much public support because of its pinpoint exposure of the misdeeds of past governments.'

'More damning is its paper on the breakdown of the billions siphoned off by the present incumbents,' said his neighbour.

'I believe its leftist agenda has caught people's imagination,' said another.

'That and *Sona munda's* promise to punish the corrupt and root out corruption.'

'Can you fault the public?' said a candidate at the further end of the table, 'it has been denied basic rights for decades … while the rulers are swilling in money … they are counted amongst the richest men worldwide, and all that's happened at the cost of the ordinary man.'

'Whose cause are we serving by this talk?' asked another. 'We represent the government in power and must take its side no matter what ... let us focus on the positive aspects of the King's party programme.'

'I think before we do that, we must assess the strengths and weaknesses of our main opponents,' said the first questioner.

'True,' Sartaj said, 'how can you campaign effectively without first trashing the rivals.'

'Downing Ameer Bakhsh Lashari should not be too difficult ... he is a greenhorn with no experience of politics or public office. The Tehreek has no notable candidate in any of the constituencies.'

'The Maulana can be attacked for the amount of time he spends on his taxicab chain business ... at the cost of his religious and political responsibilities. After all he's not called "Maulana Taxi" for nothing.'

'The difficulty we face is in finding a strategy to get at Princess Bisma.'

'She has entered politics,' Sartaj said, 'and must be treated like any other political opponent.'

'Since she has no political record, I suppose we can refer to her lack of experience.'

'I'm sure if we searched, we would find some information or involvement that can be used against her.'

'You must not be disrespectful or personal in your references to her,' Behr-e-Karam cautioned.

There was a pause.

'We are aware of her position ... and of course, we'll be most courteous even with barbs and sarcasm.'

'Perhaps you should clear what you plan to say with us before making it public,' Behr-e-Karam suggested.

'Of course Prince ...I think that's a good idea,' a candidate said looking round the table.

Many of his fellow candidates murmured their concurrence. Sartaj feigned indifference.

A telephone nearby startled everyone by its shrill ringing tone. Mehboob Alam leapt to answer it. Moments later he handed the receiver to Sartaj and whispered in his ear. It was the minister of the interior calling from the capital. Sartaj spoke confirming that the meeting with candidates was underway and that all issues were being addressed. Replacing the receiver, he instructed the stenographer and recordists to leave the room. Mehboob Alam shut the door behind them.

'Let's now discuss the most important part of the election strategy,' Sartaj said almost conspiratorially. 'What methods for controlling the balloting process are proposed to ensure your success?'

There was a pause. The candidates exchanged glances.

'Polling officers have been picked from school teachers who can be influenced,' a candidate said.

'Are they partial to us.? Will they do what is required?'Sartaj enquired.

'They are official employees serving in government schools located in our constituencies.'

'How can you be sure that they will rig the ballot boxes as told?' Sartaj enquired. 'You won't be there to oversee their actions.'

'They reside in our areas … they've been spoken to and most have agreed to do as directed.'

'Your Highness, these fellows were polling officers in past elections. They're familiar with the requirements … in all those elections they rigged in favour of the government party candidates,' an older candidate said reassuringly.

'So long as you all know how important the polling officer is for success in the election,' Sartaj emphasised. 'Now what is the position of the voters' lists?'

'Not much we can do there … they are carried over from the last election … but at least we have some idea of the numbers of dummy entries on the lists.'

'Votes equivalent to approximations of these entries, minus ten percent, marked in your favour must be prepared and cast into ballot boxes by polling officers before the voting starts,' Sartaj advised.

'That will be done, Highness.'

'As soon as polling stops, the polling officers will add up the total number of votes cast … which are not expected to be more than fifty percent of the aggregate votes in a constituency … thumb prints will then be rubber stamped on voter slips equivalent in number to the uncast votes, favouring King's party candidates and inserted in the ballot boxes.'

This has to be done double quick before the ballot boxes are taken away by security for counting.'

'I trust all polling officers have been primed accordingly,' Sartaj remarked looking round.

'All … all … Your Highness.'

The Tehreek-e-Awam went along with Ameer Bakhsh's scheme to contest two, but not three constituencies. The party election managers felt it was risky putting up three security deposits for a single candidate whose success was not assured.

Nor were they agreeable to the notion of depriving another party hopeful of the opportunity to contest from the third constituency which Ameer Bakhsh sought for himself. He had to accept that ruling for good reason – the Tehreek was bearing the expenses of his campaign.

Ameer Bakhsh got busy with the pre-election groundwork earlier than other candidates. He was aware of the yawning difference between him and them. They were favoured by Deriabad capital interests – feudals, landed gentry, religious strongholds, trade and industry. Most of them were known to the voting public. His appeal had low rating – humble trappings and a track record of Tehreek sponsored welfare service in tandem with NGOs in low income areas.

To enhance his image, he put together a masterly report with the help of Tehreek publicists. In it the nation's problems were listed, exacerbation of the problems by misgovernance of past regimes was highlighted, remedial measures proposed by the Tehreek were discussed, socio-political objectives of the party were explained and his political philosophy expounded.

The report found its way into areas where little was known about him. This was followed by corner meetings in populated localities, seminars or question and answer forums at centres of education, labour, commerce and industry and talk sessions wherever he could get in. Coverage of his involvement in social welfare work also featured on television. He planned to top this, close to the polling date with a mass meeting addressed by his leader, retired Air Vice Marshal Changez Khan Turkmanzai, disparagingly referred to as *Sona munda* by the National Front.

Behr-e-Karam's cellphone rang persistently. He had forgotten to take it with him when he went on shikar with his house guests from the port city. His wife, sensing an air of urgency about the calls picked it up finally. The call was from the capital. She pressed the receiver button on an impulse and was instantly exposed to Major Tariq's repeated 'hellos.' She was inclined for moment to switch off, but instead found herself responding to the anxious sounding caller.

'My husband is away. He is expected back this evening,' she explained.

'Please tell him that Major Tariq called …he should get in touch with me on getting back.'

When told on his return, Behr-e-Karam muttered crossly, 'Why doesn't he call in the evenings as he's been told to do. The morning calls are most inconvenient.'

He strode into his study and called the Major, who answered promptly.

*Probably standing to attention and clicking his heels,* Behr-e-Karam thought. Before he could speak, the Major raised a question about the meeting between Sartaj and the King's party candidates.

'Why wasn't I informed of this earlier?' he asked. 'My superiors knew about it, before I did. In fact *they* informed me that such a meeting had taken place.'

'I was going to tell you about it after the weekend,' Behr-e-Karam said lamely, caught off guard.

'Such information should be passed on as soon as it happens, if not in its planning stage. Delayed information can become meaningless … please bear that in mind Prince.'

'Yes Major,' Behr-e-Karam mumbled.

'Kindly tell me what matters were discussed, the names of the participants, decisions if any made and who were the lead speakers.'

Behr-e-Karam dithered, so the Major said,

'If you find it difficult to report on the information at this time, please record your response on the device I sent and forward the spool by courier.'

'That suits me better.' Behr-e-Karam said, relieved.

'Apart from the election plans what other matters of special interest were raised?'

'Well … reference was made to three of the major contestants – Ameer Bakhsh Lashari from the Tehreek-e-Awam, Maulana Anwarullah from the Jamaat-e-Muslimeen and Princess Bisma Sultan as an independent candidate.'

'We are specially interested in developments regarding these three … can your recall what was said?'

'Let me see … there was a brief discussion on strategy to oppose them.'

'What was said about Princess Bisma?'

'Not much … except that they would have to unearth some negative information to use against her.'

'Was there any talk about disfiguring the votes polled in favour of the opponents?'

'I don't think so … but the manoeuvering of votes and voters' lists by polling officers was discussed in some detail.'

'Thank you Prince for the information. I shall await the spool. Don't mind my saying so, but please be on the ball from now on.'

Behr-e-Karam did not respond. He felt put down.

'What's the matter *jani?*' his wife asked when he came out of the study.

'It's these dratted agency men. They expect too much.'

'Why do you let them get to you? Just tell them that you are not answerable to officialdom.'

He wished he could have said as much to Major Tariq but the yoke taken on for coinage held him back from doing so.

# Chapter 11

'Every person has the right to choose the kind of life he wants to lead …' were the first words Bisma uttered after the traditional invocation to Allah, 'but it is the circumstances governing one's existence that determine what kind of life one ultimately gets to lead.'

It was sundown in Shahryar Peoples Park. The crowd – the largest ever seen in Deriabad – stirred, intrigued by the sight of an Umrani princess launching her electoral campaign from a raised stage in a public park. Banners and flags bearing her name rippled in the evening breeze.

*There's something about her,* Ameer Bakhsh noted observing the tall, regal figure draped in white from his vantage point.

'The poor and the underprivileged,' she stressed, raising her arms in the direction of the crowd, 'have no option but to lead lives shaped by the blighted circumstances controlling their existence. Freedom of choice is snatched from them before birth … they are prisoners of a system like fish in a pond or animals caged in a zoo …' the well modulated tones rose ringingly '…most people in our country are denied this choice … they are condemned to lives devoid of hope.'

An air of expectancy was discernible in the crowd.

'But there are some … some of us who by accident of birth or by achieving economic success, get into a position to straddle the system, to rise above it. Some of these people achieve power for controlling communities. Because of their power, they also tend to gravitate into the ranks of the ruling class of a nation. They are then able to make the system their creature … to manipulate it to suit their purposes, which may be good or bad.'

A murmur rose at the extremities and travelled in rising decibels towards the center of the gathering, disseminating in waves around the stage.

*She's got to them* Ameer Bakhsh thought. *Clever woman ... she must sense the effect she's having.*

The floodlights were switched on suddenly, banishing the shades of dusk as if touched by a wand. The crowd blinked. The illumination highlighted the solitary speaker on stage, upright as beacon, the pale face framed by a white veil mirrored in the eyes of watchers.

'By taking part in this election, I have had to cast aside a family precedent which forbids Umranis from entering politics. I have had to flout the traditional purdah worn by my family by appearing thus ...' arms outstretched, 'before the people of Deriabad. I have done this to get access to the circles where the policies of government are made. I have done this so that I may get a chance to strike at the system that enslaves our people ...'

'Shahzadi Bisma Sultan zindabad,' was intoned by a single voice in the crowd. It became a signal for recurrent 'zindabads' resounding across the park amidst waving flags and fluttering banners.

*Now she has them,* Ameer Bakhsh concluded. *Must hand it to you Princess. If I were in the crowd I too would've cheered.*

'I do not represent the ruling family here nor am I a member of any political party, nor do I have a political agenda. I stand as one person dependent on your support for representing your interests in the Assembly of those who will discuss national policies and make laws imposing those policies.'

'Bibi, how will you bring about the changes in policies?' a voice from the crowd called out.

'I don't claim to be powerful enough to change government policies on my own. I will be only one voice in an assembly of over three hundred and forty members but I shall make my voice heard by calling out for the inclusion of people friendly measures in the policy proposals coming before the National Assembly. Such measures may or may not be acceptable to the policy makers, but my views will be preserved in the record of the proceedings ...if I speak out loud enough and often enough, other like minded members of the Assembly will take up the call.

Of those who will be elected, a sufficient number have undertaken to join me in a citizens rights group which will lobby the electors for promoting human rights in the laws passed by the National Assembly ... most of them are persons of influence from different parts of the country who have watched the degradation of our people year after year on account of the disastrous policies of the governments of the last fifty years. They have observed the corruption and the mismanagement of the ruling classes and feel as I do that the rot must be stopped. So we have one agenda, and that is to bring about change by applying pressure in the National Assembly.

If our amendments to the laws being made are rejected, we will draft our own set of rules and present them in private members bills to be enacted as laws. If we fail to bring about people friendly changes in the self seeking, distorted political climate it will result in revolution, destruction, terrorism ... and violence of a kind worse then that witnessed in Iraq, Syria and Nigeria.'

The words magnified by the sound system rang out over an attentive crowd.

*Simple truths ... true words ... strength of conviction,* Ameer Bakhsh mused.

'We may not succeed in our endeavours, but we will carry on regardless ... it may take years for our influence to blend into government policy ... but if our movement persists from one election to the next and the next, the essence of what we struggle for will ultimately seep into the culture of policy making.'

Another round of 'zindabads' led by cheer leaders went up, and would have continued if Bisma had not raised her hands for attention.

'My father served his people when he was ruler of Deriabad State, and even later when the state became part of the country.'

More cheering and cries of 'Nawab Shahryar Alam Khan zindabad,' '*Naara e takbeer* – Allah hu Akbar.'

'Like him, I will serve you and stand up for your rights as I would for my own. To help me fulfil this commitment, I need your support

...' then by a flick of hand she swept the chadar off her shoulders and held it out as if seeking alms.

'Will you support me?' she asked before casting the chadar down on the dais, standing exposed and vulnerable.

In the ensuing silence Almas leapt on stage, wrapped the chadar round Bisma and led her away.

Ameer Bakhsh held his breath and gaped in disbelief. The crowd, momentarily immobile, surged and heaved like a tidal mass, then went berserk. Cries of 'Bibi we are with you,' 'We will be your protectors,' 'We will die for you,' 'Princess Bisma zindabad, zindabad, you are the pride of Deriabad,' rent the air.

The roar spread far and wide, reverberating like distant thunder in the halls of Falaktaj Palace.


'Well, she's done it,' Kulsoom said, 'displaying herself in the Peoples Park in front of all those men, begging for their help ...'

'Bhabijan please,' Behr-e-Karam, said, 'let's focus on the fallout of her speech instead of irrelevancies.'

'Why irrelevancies Bhai?' Kulsoom remarked ignoring his caution. 'Removing the dupatta and showing her body to strangers is what a dancing girl does, not a princess ...'

'Shut up,' Badshah Begum said, 'you heard Behr-e-Karam.'

'I'm only telling you what people are saying,' Kulsoom persisted.

'You have a foul mouth Kulsoom. Besides, you distort facts.'

'Amma Huzoor' Sartaj cried out in protest.

'Well, its true,' Badshah Begum said, 'everybody knows what actually happened in the park and what people have to say about it, but trust Kulsoom to give it her spin.'

'Bisma's public appearance is against the interests of the family,' Sartaj said.

'Maybe so, but does it help to have Kulsoom's slanderous comments bandied about as the family view on Bisma's politics?'

'Let's take a step back,' Behr-e-Karam said, 'and try being objective.'

'Quite so,' Badshah Begum said. 'Must say though that her entry into politics was quite dramatic.'

'At the risk of running afoul of Bhabijan, I think it was spectacular,' Behr-e-Karam said laughingly.

'What is the reaction in Deriabad?' Sartaj asked scowling.

'Most people were surprised at her coming out like that but they are very supportive … I think many will vote for her,' Behr-e-Karam said.

'*Tamasha,* that's all it is … people get excited by a good looking woman from the topmost family making a public spectacle of herself,' Kulsoom put in.

'You wouldn't say that Ammi if you had been there,' Sartaj's elder son said.

'Were you there?' Behr-e-Karam asked.

'Yes, Uncle, I was,' he murmured quietly.

'How could you?' Kulsoom retorted, rounding on him.

'It's alright,' Sartaj remarked, 'I told him to go, see and report back to me.'

'Without telling me?'

'Kulsoom, cut out the melodrama,' Badshah Begum said. 'We have important things to discuss and your spiteful comments keep getting in the way.'

They continued talking, aware that the political perspective had changed. The implications would be assessed at the capital by the interested parties. In Deriabad they would have some effect on the nawab's status and the interests of other family members. It was time for the Umranis to do some soul searching.

Behr-e-Karam spoke to Major Tariq on Skype about the rally soon after it had taken place. He was anxious to avoid further charges of tardiness. The Major had however, received earlier reports of the event from his other sources.

'We want factual information of reactions from nawab sahib's inner group, and from Deriabad business circles,' the Major said.

'The palace is worried. Nawab Sartaj sees it as an intrusion in his sphere of influence,' Behr-e-Karam said. He went on to give an account of the discussion with Sartaj, coming up short when he saw on Skype that the Major was recording his comments.

*These spooks,* he thought, *they're creepy.*

The views of the business community would have to wait until Behr-e-Karam could access them.

A few days later, Major Tariq was called to a meeting at the federal capital of the think-tank that dealt, among other matters, with the internal security of the nation. The participants included senior army officers each representing a security agency and Lieutenant General Altaf Sarfaraz representing the secret service. They were assisted by the ministers of the interior and defence, essential bureaucrats, a handful of colonels and a brigadier or two who specialized in covert activities.

'We should finalize our approach to the elections before the next meeting of the corp. commanders,' said chief of a security agency.

'Looks like we have reached agreement with our friends in government,' General Altaf Sarfaraz said glancing at the executives present, 'on ways for handling most of the constituencies. A few trouble spots remain in some of the federating units.'

The ministers nodded agreement. Major Tariq consulted his notes and identified seventeen constituencies that required special attention.

'Three are especially troublesome,' he said, 'Jamkot, Ranipur and Deriabad.'

'I agree with your assessment Tariq,' one of the generals said. 'We have to find some special solutions that may be workable just for them … what we propose for the others are not appropriate for this lot.'

'I would suggest, sir,' Major Tariq said, 'that we should first determine a course of action for the fourteen less problematic constituencies before dealing with these three.'

During the discussion, sandwiches and coffee were served for lunch. By teatime they were appraising what measures were required for controlling the electoral results of the three problem constituencies.

'The Ranipur and Jamkot circumstances are somewhat alike … and the outcome predictable,' the defence minister said, 'so similar controls should work for both of them … but Deriabad hmmm …'

'Deriabad,' said the interior minister, 'will require careful handling. If the popular vote favours the princess, as most of the analysts predict, our plans must be foolproof.'

'I would say, minister,' Lieutenant General Altaf Sarfaraz remarked, 'that they should not be traceable back to us. It would create an almighty stink against our groups, but something clearly must be done to prevent Princess Bisma from succeeding. Her entry to the National Assembly would consolidate the citizens rights group that has been warming its backside for the last few months.'

'Who are the main supporters of this movement?' the defence minister asked.

'I know of the group leaders, Pir Sahib of Rehbar Sharif, Dr. Jasmin Jalal and Altmash Arbab – all certain to be re-elected. Apart from them, who else is there?' one of the bureaucrats asked Major Tariq.

'Sir, there are thirty-two persons who have signed a memorandum of agreement they put together on their policy objectives. If they are elected, they will form a forward bloc.' Major Tariq said.

'Are all of them likely to be elected?' General Altaf asked.

'Most of them are dead certs,' the interior minister said, 'but the leaders of the movement are the dangerous ones ... they have a programme to take on the existing order in the Assembly by speeches, motions and legislative manouevres, and also out of the Assembly by strikes, seminars and *dharnas*. They have chalked out an aggressive programme. From what I understand, there is no stopping this lot.'

'Why do you say that?' the defence minister asked.

'It seems that they have public backing. Ironically, they all are feudals or vested interests, so they are well known in their areas. Some have national and international significance. Most are academically qualified. There are professionals among them too. Some hold prominent posts.'

'Dyed in wool nationalists,' the defence minister said.

'Exactly,' the interior minister replied, 'not to be deflected from what they think is good for the country.'

'Then may be it's not such a bad thing if they get elected,' one of colonels murmured.

'Even if they disrupt the existing balance of power?' Major Tariq asked.

'If the national interest comes first for them, perhaps they should get a chance.'

'Colonel, you seem to have lost your mind.' General Altaf bristled. 'You're overlooking what we have accomplished. We know what's good for the country from years of experience. We know the ground rules, the nuts and bolts, the ideology, the faith. We have given our lives for the nation. Do you think these jokers are more dedicated than us?'

'Sorry sir, I didn't mean it that way.'

'Minister Sahib,' General Altaf addressed the interior minister, 'is there any way to check these people from pursuing their agenda?'

'How do you mean, General?'

'By applying the persuasion usually reserved for such situations.'

'I don't think so, General. They are wealthy and influential. Not looking for material benefits, posts or cookies … for the sake of power. They are also unlikely to be deterred by threats or sanctions. Whoever has got them together, has done a masterful job.'

'Crappy do-gooders,' General Altaf said scornfully, 'who'll disrupt the system … not straight away, but bit by bit, if given time. They will create chaos and blame us for all that is bad. Then it'll be difficult to control any mass movement. They must be stopped now. It's time to draw up our strategy for dealing with these termites.'

# Chapter 12

Soon after Sadie's engagement to Hussain, Ninette and the princesses left for Paris to purchase trousseau items. The wedding was scheduled just before the elections.

They were received at Orly airport by the Deriabad agent in France. Ninette's pied-a-terre was on Avenne Foch. It was a modern, spacious apartment with a hint of tradition in the trompe l'oeil frescoes. A fortyish housekeeper called Simone let them in with a welcoming smile.

Ninette ordered coffee, scanned a local newspaper and placed orders for invitations to fashion shows and tickets for plays, the opera and cinema shows. While sipping coffee she made a list of select shops and department stores. Sartaj had provided some funds for the trousseau. Knowing that he was unlikely to make up shortfalls, she instructed the agent to get cheque books and pay orders from her banks. 'You're like a whirlwind Mummy,' Sadie said, 'We've just got here and wooosh you're off again.'

'Time is short. We can't waste any,' she shot back.

The next day, the shopping extravaganza got underway.

Fashionwear, winter wear, undergarments, shoes, cosmetics, household items were tackled zestfully. The mornings started off with expectations and the evenings ended in exhaustion. The shows provided some relief to aching backs and sore feet.

An unexpected visitor turned up before they set out one morning. Simone announced that a Monsieur Arnaud, legal advisor to the late ruler – accompanied by the Deriabad agent – wished to pay respects.

'As you are aware Your Highness,' Monsieur Arnaud said ponderously, 'His Highness had invested in French and Swiss securities and in urban and commercial properties in France.'

'Why are you discussing these matters with me? His Highness' successor, Nawab Sartaj Umrani is the right person to approach,' Ninette said.

'Quite so, we have kept Nawab Sartaj informed about progress in the transfer of title in these interests to the ruler's heirs. The French court gave a decision a few days ago of which Nawab Sartaj has been informed.

'Well then, the matter is settled.'

'There is more Your Highness that concerns you.'

'Me?' Ninette exclaimed.

'Yes, Highness. Nawab Sahib's financial transactions were handled by the Banque Credit de Marseilles. They were not simply his bankers and investment managers but also custodians of items he left with them for safekeeping.'

'Yes, yes,' Ninette said, anxious to get back to the shoppers waiting impatiently in the wings

'One such item was a box so long,' he held out his hands eighteen inches apart, 'about ten inches high, with a key in a sealed envelope … this was to be delivered to you on his death.'

'Odd,' Ninette remarked, 'he never mentioned it to me.'

'Well, court orders giving access of the box to Your Highness have come through. We should therefore go to the bank to take possession.

'Do you have any idea what's in it?'

'No, Your Highness … except his remark when depositing the box that it held answers to some family riddles.'

The next morning Ninette and Monsieur Arnaud called at the baroque premises of the three hundred year old bank. In a reception hall with a vaulted ceiling, Gerard Duplessis, suave, tanned, and greying haired President of the bank bowed low over Ninette's hand. 'Begum, I have had the honour of attending to your late husband during his visits to Paris, and look forward to serving you and your family.'

He led the way to a locker room where he unlocked a cabinet and withdrew from it an attaché case sized carved wooden chest with a sealed key cover. Ninette took charge and signed an acknowledgement.

Back in the apartment, she opened the chest in her bedroom. The upper compartment contained four scrolls inscribed with Arabic, Persian, Urdu and Devanagari texts and separate sheets containing rough English translations of some texts. One of them contained a history of the Umrani family from its founding up to the nineteenth century. The early writing was in Arabic, the later in Persian. Another contained a tangled family tree of the Umranis effective up to the nineteenth century. The third, an itemised account in Persian and Urdu of the burial sites of Umrani rulers who were not interred at the Deriabad graveyard.

The fourth – which when fully unrolled, was sizable – depicted a terrain containing representations of landmarks extending along a sketchy route traversing from Falaktaj Palace which was identified by the state flag at the bottom left of the scroll to a domed structure marked by a swastika located in the top right section of what appeared like the Satrang desert.

The landmarks, comprising hills, woodlands, rocky outcrops, watercourses and settlements, identified in crude Arabic or Devanagari scripts, ended at the domed structure. There were lengthy notations at the end of the scroll in the Devanagari. The borders of the scroll were embossed with swastikas.

Three slim cases, inscribed to Bisma Sultan, Sadia Sultan and Rabia Sultan lay in the lower section of the chest. Each contained a pendant of a faceted pearshaped diamond suspended from strands inlaid with diamonds. The faceted diamond being sizable, was set in enamelled gold casing the reverse of which bore a miniature representation of the ruler. There were also three pouches for the begums. Each contained a rosary of matched uncut stones which included emeralds, rubies and sapphires.

A few days later an impressive floral arrangement and a box of liqueur chocolates were delivered to the apartment. Gerard Duplessis had sent them with an invitation to the opera and dinner. Ninette was in two minds about accepting. So she consulted Monsieur Arnaud, who advised her to go.

Gerard Duplessis also invited Sheikh Jassim bin Ahmed Al-Thani of Qatar, to join Ninette with both princesses in the box. During the performance, Ninette could feel Gerard's eyes on her. When it ended, she sought to get away but was persuaded by Gerard and Shaikh Jassim to dine with them at Maxim's. After dinner, Sheikh Jassim suggested a visit to the casino.

Ninette did not want to extend the evening further. Gerard succeeded in overcoming her reluctance by indicating that it would be an exciting new experience for the princesses. They were quite thrilled at the prospect. It had been a memorable evening – first the opera, then Maxim's and now the casino. They did not want it to end. Ninette knew she was beaten. Her reluctance was more a ploy to avoid Gerard's attentions than concern for the girls' welfare. What harm could there be in letting them visit the casino.

The Aviation Club de France on Champs-Elysees was a vertitable wonderland for the uninitiated. Betting was in full swing when they walked in. Gerard excused himself and went off to play Baccarat. Sheikh Jassim chose the game of Le Multicolore. It was being played on a large gaming table. A white ivory ball struck by the croupier rolled tantalizingly towards the colourful wheel of fortune at the centre settling ultimately on one of the colours.

The Sheikh asked Ninette to stay with him for good luck. The princesses wandered off to watch the action elsewhere. His luck that evening was phenomenal. Whichever colour he placed his chips on turned up as a winner. News of his winning streak travelled round the casino causing many punters to flock to the table where his pile of chips multiplied with each roll of the ball. It was a day for fate to take control. The end came inevitably by a turn that broke the bank.

Onlookers cheered and champagne corks popped when Sheikh Jassim came out of the manager's office, cheque in hand. He seemed to be walking on air. Gerard was somewhat inebriated by then. Much whisky had been downed while he watched the Sheikh play. Some of the Middle Easterners present were galvanized into a celebratory mood on account of the triumph against odds of one of their kind.

Paparazzi always alert for sensational items, sensed an opportunity to extract something from the story of the evening. They would have to wait for Sheikh Jassim to leave before moving in because house rules forbade coverage on the premises.

Sheikh Jassim announced on the sound system that anyone who wished to celebrate his success should follow him home. There was a general scramble for cars.

Sheikh Jassim swung his Bugati sportscar round and asked Ninette to jump in. She hesitated.

'Come on lady,' he said, 'I'm not letting you go. You brought me good luck. Don't desert me now.'

Ninette looked round wildly for the girls, pushing them onto the back seat of the four-seater before getting in beside the Sheikh.

Gerard followed in his Aston Martin. The Sheikh led with an almighty acceleration prompting the merrymakers, including Americans, Arabs, French and Germans to give chase. After half an hour of speeding up and down city roads – during which Sheikh Jassim was unmoved by Ninette's pleas to slow down – the cars wound up zooming round and round the Place de la Concorde. Then inexplicably, Sheikh Jassim veered towards Pont de la Concorde and crossed over the Seine to the Left Bank.

Fate stepped in again when the lead car got on to Quay Voltaire. Midway along the embankment it came suddenly upon a road sweeper that had been left stranded without warning lights. The noise of the crash disturbed pigeons roosting in buildings half a kilometer away. Cars in pursuit swerved wildly – brakes shrieking – to avoid the wreck and ended up hitting something or the other. Those who failed to brake or braked too late piled into the first car. Some vaulted over smouldering scraps of metal hitting the embankment railing.

Sheikh Jassim was killed on the spot. Gerard Duplessis suffered a broken spine, fractures and a smashed face. Four others died and many were hideously injured. Miraculously nothing happened to the road sweeper or Ninette and the princesses save for the after-effects of shock. Most of the cars were write-offs. Some were reduced to cinders. The accident site looked like a blitzed junkyard and smelled of roasted rubber days after the event.

The paparazzi slavouring like hyenas, had a field day. For them the Dowager Begum of Deriabad, two princesses, Sheikh Jassim bin Ahmed Al-Thani of Qatar, President Gerard Duplessis of the Banque Credit de Marseilles and other notables amounted to a heady collection of celebrities involved in the worst car crash seen in Paris.

News with vivid coverage of the smash-up and the people involved, reached Deriabad on the BBC and CNN channels within an hour of the event. Shock sustained by disbelief that such an unseemly event involving the Umranis in Paris had happened, coupled with embarrassment and anger were not confined to Sartaj. They were experienced in varying degrees by other members of the family too.

Kulsoom never had such opportunity to spew venom, nor to bemoan the scandalization of the Umranis. Her deadliest barbs were reserved for Ninette. She did not hesitate even to cast aspersions on the princesses.

To deal with the situation, Meheryar at Sartaj's instance, flew to Paris. There was a great deal he had to do. It took time to resolve matters concerning the Umrani ladies' involvement in the accident.

To avoid the paparazzi hounding them whenever they stepped out, the trousseau shopping had to be abandoned. There was no escape however, from the cameras arrayed at the entrance to the court conducting the enquiry on the accidental deaths. Ninette and the girls deposed in court what they had declared earlier to the police. Some venturesome newshounds even landed in Deriabad seeking local colour for their reports.

# Chapter 13

Malik Azad Khan of Mazarian Wali was by nature a sore loser. More galling was the prospect of losing his home constituency to a peasant from elsewhere. All markers indicated that the Mazarian Wali ballot was for the taking by Ameer Bakhsh Lashari.

As landowner supremo he felt that the *zamindari* code necessitated a redressal of honour by downing Ameer Bakhsh somehow. He went about engaging paid activists to campaign vociferously for National Front nominees in all Deriabad constituencies. Giant billboards displaying the contenders en famille or surrounded by supporters like the star cast of a local movie, were installed statewide. Egged on by the police, Ameer Bakhsh's meetings were mired by catcalls and abrasive hecklers. His posters and banners were blackened or shredded.

Word of the vandalism soon reached Sartaj. He assumed that Malik Azad had been put up to this by the National Front or government agencies. When he learnt the real reason at a town hall meeting of pro-government candidates, he urged Malik Azad to extend his forays to Bisma's campaign.

Somewhat taken back, Malik Azad could only murmur, '*Saeen*, Ameer Bakhsh Lashari is being taught a lesson for challenging my status. But I can't even consider opposing Princess Bisma Sultan, even though I support the National Front candidates. I could never, never take a stance against your family.'

Ameer Bakhsh and his youthful supporters were unfazed by Malik Azad's tactics. 'What more do we have to fear after the attack in Mazarian

Wali bazaar?' His motorcycle riders were undaunted in setting up corner meetings, leading rallies, distributing pamphlets, unfurling banners everywhere. It got to a point where stray motorcyclists not involved with the politicking in motion took to racing Ameer Bakhsh's riders when they zipped off on the campaign trail. The experience exposed some of the racebugs to the thrill of campaigning. Within weeks, the group had grown into a two wheeled brigade that moved like a swarm through city environs. When the riders picked their way through wheat fields, village boys gave chase crying, '*Sona munda di sawari.*' When they swept into town, policeman gave them a wide berth and outdoor tea stallers cleared their tables when they stopped by for a cuppa.

Bisma's campaign was not as meticulously planned as Ameer Bakhsh's. The Tehreek-e-Awam strategists felt that their multilayered programme would provide Ameer Bakhsh with the widespread exposure which was vital for success. This did not arise in Bisma's case as she was well known in Deriabad. Besides, the understated approach she had adopted was more in keeping with her gender and status.

She traversed her constituencies addressing low key meetings in educational institutions. For occasional public appearances – which people clamoured for – she was usually accompanied by guest speakers who included celebrated writers, moderate Islamists and social welfare or sports luminaries. Her call for the cleansing of the system of governance struck a chord with listeners. Her proposal for bringing about inductive changes in the law made sense to many save vested interests.

Ameer Bakhsh also spoke of change, though not in modulated tones. The style was flamboyant, the rhetoric declamatory. The voice touched frenzied decibels. Arms flailed the air. The words assailed the incumbent ruling class, alluding in passing to combating the entrenched order, if not to revolution. The climax came invariably with a rousing call for deductive change superimposed on the existing governance.

While Bisma's public appearances drew wage earners, artisans and small traders, Ameer Bakhsh's meetings were a major attraction for young people. Girls in particular were seen in large numbers pushing their way to the front drawn by the promise of a dashing presence and subtle virility.

'Comes in my dreams,' said a young lady.

'To die for,' said another, not so young.

'Take my vote and take my heart,' said a third.

'And what else can he take?' the last speaker was asked.

'Don't be gross,' she squealed.

Razia stood near enough to hear such remarks. They were distressing. His popularity was anathema to her. It was distancing him from her. *These women look so special,* she thought marvelling at their swirling attire and ringletted honey blonde hair extensions. Public exposure had made Ameer Bakhsh conscious of his affect on audiences. Female adulation was something new, but initial self consciousness had given way to bluff nonchalance when faced with gushing overtures. The Tehreek strategists were quick to point to the advantage of sex appeal at public rallies.

Ameer Bakhsh could sense how much Razia hated his involvement with electioneering. It kept him from her – closeted at night with the planners and gone by day on the campaign trail. Their married life had come to a standstill. His sexual activism had been subsumed by the demands of the campaign, which was far more exciting. *There will be time afterwards,* he told himself, but something kept him from believing that.

'That woman there in the black abaya who is present at all his functions, who is she?' Malik Azad Khan's overseer asked a policeman on duty.

'Oh the one there, that's his wife.'

To cover the electioneering process, the Tasveer-e-Watan TV channel had sent camera crews headed by an anchor person known nationwide. Sameera Rehman, a twenty five year old postgraduate in oriental studies had specialised in audio-visuals at UCLA and was as effective behind the camera as she was in front of it.

Sameera had a special interest in Deriabad. One of her ancestors had been in charge of the palace guard in the 1870s when Sufi Saeen ruled. During his tenure, some important artifacts and relics were stolen from the palace by four brigands who escaped southward into the Satrangi desert. At the ruler's behest a patrol from the British Indian army was sent to hunt them down. To make amends for any lapse, Sameera's ancestor had insisted on accompanying the patrol. Two dispatches sent later by Deriabad state scouts reported on the movement of the patrol deep in the desert. After that there was no news on its movements. It seemed to have disappeared in the desert.

She was naturally curious about Deriabad and hoped to find time during the assignment to discover something about the missing patrol. To get the job of covering Deriabad, she had to fall back on tenacity which helped her fend off senior presenters who had an eye on the same assignment. All of them were quite intrigued by the interesting mix of Deriabad candidates.

Having heard of the success of Bisma's inaugural public meeting, Sameera followed her to all her sites, until she came across Ameer Bakhsh. Then she was torn between the two. The matter was resolved when, at her persistence, another camera crew headed by her friend Xerxes Khambata turned up. Between them they managed to cover most of the campaigning of Bisma, Ameer Bakhsh and the National Front heavyweights.

When she was not engaged in trailing the campaigners, Sameera searched for information on the last patrol. On one occasion she was stopped from trespassing into the museum store containing uncatalogued items. If Prince Meheryar, who happened to be present at the time squiring foreign visitors, had not intervened, she may have faced charges.

Her next encounter with Meheryar was on the ferry which carried passengers between the shore and the Royal Daryadar Hunting Lodge located in the centre of Lake Umrani. It had been built by Artful Arbab, an ancestor entombed at the royal graveyard. An obvious tourist stopover, it also served high tea to visitors. Meheryar was with his guests when Sameera's camera crew hustled on to the boat just as it revved up for the trip to the lodge. She recognized the profile that gazed upon the waters of the lake.

For candidate coverage, Ameer Bakhsh's interview was conducted by Sameera at his home in Pattanwala, and at the Tehreek office in town. She showed special interest in the coverage of the Mazarian Wali skirmish which had been caught on cellular phone by a quick-on-the-draw spectator. Her searching questions on his contest with Princess Bisma and the National Front incumbents fitted aptly into her TV programme entitled, 'Tilting at Windmills.'

Ameer Bakhsh parried the irony in the peasant versus princess contest, but responded sturdily when questioned about his views on the National Front worthies.'Not at all intimidated, is he?' Sameera observed to Xerxes.

Bisma was interviewed at her home, with her workers in the campaign office, electioneering in community environs, and finally within the grandeur of Falaktaj Palace. For the final portion of the interview, Bisma was flanked by her brother, Meheryar in formal surroundings. She made a strong case for the citizens rights programme backed by slides on the works in hand.

Later, at the tea table Sameera asked Meheryar, 'Are you really to the manner born?'

'If you are asking whether I belong to the family ... well, yes I do.'

'An Umrani, true blue?'

'Who did you think I was?'

'A palace official.'

'Near enough I suppose.'

'Sorry Prince, or Highness, I should've guessed – such a good looking family. I'll know better next time.'

'The name is Meheryar,' he said with a smile.

'Honoured,' Sameera said biting into a sandwich.

Aren't you a TV celebrity?'

'One has to make a living.'

'I mean you're fairly well known. People seem to like your programmes.'

'I didn't think you would've noticed.'

'Come on, do you think I live on the moon?'

'Perhaps not the moon Prince, but there is something dystopic about Deriabad.' After another bite, she said 'Wasn't there an item on world news about Deriabad lately?'

'What are you referring to?' Meheryar asked, stiffening.

'It had something to do with – to do with – yes, I remember now – that car crash in Paris involving the foreign begum and some princesses.'

'What of it?' Meheryar said brushing the matter off.

'That was quite something. The opera, Maxime's, the casino and the crash.'

'Newshound's dream coverage,' Meheryar spat out.

'People, as I said, have to make a living, Prince – most of us are not born with silver spoons.'

'I didn't mean it that way. I was referring to the lurid build up, the innuendo.'

'Face facts Prince, it was a great story – staggering events, glamorous personages, royalty caught in unusual settings, overtones of scandal, international flavouring – what more could a newsman ask for?'

'Let's drop the subject,' Meheryar said frowning.

'I'm sorry Prince. I didn't intend to offend you.'

'Well, you were talking about my family.'

'Not disrespectfully sir, more like pointing out that the item became a hit on account of the involvement of royalty in a colossal smash-up of umpteen cars.'

'Meheryar put his teacup down and walked away.

*Oops, I seem to've crossed him,* Sameera thought.

Somewhat mortified, she turned to chat with Bisma all the while following Meheryar out of corner of her eye. Unable to hold back, she made her way to where he stood, tapped him on the shoulder and said, 'Sir, my remarks were rhetorical, not personal. If I've gone too far …'

'Stop right there,' Meheryar said, a disarming smile spreading across his face. 'I fear I have overreacted to what – as you said – were rhetorical references to my family. So no offence was meant and none taken.'

Sameera smiled back, somewhat self-consciously.

To reset the ball rolling, Meheryar asked, 'How long have you been a media person?'

'Almost three years now.'

'You don't look old enough.'

'I started out teaching audio-visuals in the performing arts faculty at the Port City university.'

'What brought you to TV?'

'An offer I could not refuse. Someone saw me on video doing a course on programme preparation …and here I am.'

After a pause Meheryar said, 'Your outfit … I mean the tights, long tunic, and the balaclava headgear ending in dupatta panels draped over shoulders… a uniform or what?'

She laughed, 'I daresay, you could call it that.'

'Don't get me wrong. I think it's very stylish but my curiosity got the better of me as I've never seen anything like it.'

It's what's referred to as on Islam conformist attire, designed to cover all that is meant to be covered, modishly of course. It's meant for Muslim females who want to avoid being mistaken for a shuttlecock or a faceless black column or a bandaged nose job case when they venture for work into the big bad world.'

'Is it effective?'

'Seems to be. It's accepted as a hijab, a sort of designer version.'

'Do the fundamentalists approve?'

'No official comment so far, but nothing women friendly has ever come from that lobby.'

'Well, I don't know.'

'No, you don't Prince. The truth is that this country is hostile territory for working women.'


A smell of incense lingered on the terrace where Sartaj, Anwar Pasha and Behr-e-Karam were strolling.

'I can't hold her back,' Anwar Pasha said, 'can you?'

'She's your wife,' Sartaj fumed.

'So?'

'Well then, it's your job.'

'You know exactly how things are, Bhai Sahib.'

'Yes, yes, but other than Meheryar, you are still in a position to talk to her about the disruption she's causing.'

'Forgive me,' Behr-e-Karam interceded, 'but what's the point of this discussion? Bisma and Anwar are not on the same page, nor have been for years. So Bhaijan, why would she listen to him on a matter as important to her as the election?'

'I am getting a lot of flak from the establishment on the publicity raised by her campaign. As if I can do something about that! I've already cautioned her about suspension of her privy purse allowance.'

'You would do that for her political activities?' Behr-e-Karam asked incredulously.

'Well, I haven't said so. If I had, she would for sure have protested to the states ministry, and they would be breathing down my neck for abuse of privilege. I've explained it more as an essential cutback because of the slashed privy purse.

'Just as you have written to tell all of us,' Behr-e-Karam said drily.

'Necessary dear brother. Don't you start now, I've had protests from the begums and sahibzadas. Some landed up at the palace unannounced.'

'What do you expect Bhai Sahib,' Anwar Pasha asked, 'When you slash lifelines?'

'Come on Anwar, you can't complain. Bisma is a rich lady, and Rani Sahib is loaded,' Sartaj said. 'You also have private sources apart from your official salary?'

'Wasn't talking about myself ... it's those dependents who are without means.'

'All growing fat on state handouts. Lazy buggers ... it'll do them good, to get off their butts and earn for themselves.'

'All right Bhaijan,' Behr-e-Karam said shortly, 'there's no need to abuse people who do not have your privileges.'

Later, leading the way into an antechamber, Sartaj remarked,

'I called this meeting to discuss Bisma's politicking and look where it has ended ... with a finger levelled at me ... which is what you people always do.'

Behr-e-Karam and Anwar Pasha exchanged glances.

'Anyway,' Sartaj continued plumping down on a sofa, 'Bisma has to stop bad mouthing the special interests. It is hitting home now. They won't put up with it much longer. Her exposure of facts and figures has left them open to serious accusations and negative comment in the public media.'

'She's not the only one,' Anwar Pasha said, 'there are others in that group too.'

'She is the ring leader … that's the way they see it,' Sartaj said. 'I'm warning you Anwar to set your home in order before they strike.'

'Bhaijan, you call Bisma and tell her yourself,' Behr-e-Karam said. 'Anwar Pasha can't do much here. I think it's already too late. Bisma has set her gunsights. She seems determined now on fulfilling her agenda. If you don't know that about her, respected brother, you don't know your sister.'

# Chapter 14

Razia felt the filming by the Tasveer-e-Watan channel was a violation of her family privacy. She resented being directed by the hooded woman in skin tight leggings and a wraparound dupatta whom Ameer Bakhsh seemed to hold in awe.

*Ridiculous,* she thought, *having to squat at the outdoor oven, tend cattle in the pen, feed the toddler on a charpoy or braid the girl's hair for school … as if that's all village women do. For all their superior airs, these city folk know nothing.*

Xerxes darted around Allah Bakhsh's habitation capturing back-up shots for Ameer Bakhsh's interview. At one stage, when Razia failed to respond to calls for joining a family shot, Ameer stomped in to fetch her. His angry tones in Seraiki were discernible over Razia's pleading to be left alone followed by the sound of a slap which shook Sameera. When, after a while, they came out, Ameer Bakhsh was scowling but the frown had been wiped off Razia's freshly washed face.

The episode was unsettling. Sameera felt it was time to wrap up. The rural scene had been sullied.

Later, when she interviewed Bisma, she detected other strains. There was a lingering trace of treachery. *Probably an after-effect of the break-up of a once perfect match,* she mused. Now barrenness and desolation pervaded the home on the hill of the beauty in waiting. Sameera had heard of Anwar Pasha's satyric profligacy. At Deriabad they spoke of Bisma's probity and even-handedness.

*Why,* she wondered, *were men so flawed in dealing with women.*

With the election fervour mounting, the think-tank entrusted with monitoring political affairs from the nation's eagle's nest, conducted a review of leading candidates. The Deriabad report identified two front runners – Bisma and Ameer Bakhsh. The think-tank's manouvering and measures to undercut Deriabad's favoured children had failed to stem their support. Faced with the shambles of the earlier policy, the planners firmed up another approach, somewhat predictably referred to as Plan B.

The guest relations manager at the Shahpasand Hotel almost skipped as he conducted Major Tariq to his suite. He recalled his earlier visit to Deriabad, and offered somewhat obsequiously, to place all his services at the Major's disposal. Behr-e-Karam had been advised of Major Tariq's visit and was told to await his arrival at the hotel. Taking exception to the brusque tone of the GHQ telephone operator who seemed oblivious to his princely status, Behr-e-Karam was tempted to snub his instructors, but given the extent to which he was implicated with the agencies, he chose instead to be prudent, and waited for the Major's call before proceeding to the hotel.

'My principals want meetings with Princess Bisma Sultan and Ameer Bakhsh Lashari,' the Major said.
'Separate meetings, I take it.'
'Yes, yes, entirely unconnected.'
'Where – here or at the capital?'
'In Deriabad of course.'
'Who will represent your principals?'
'Some senior offiers. I'm not sure who.'
'I can understand your seeking my help for meeting my sister, but I'm damned if I'm getting involved with the Lashari chap.'
'I understand your reluctance, Prince. We didn't mean offence. Just wondered whether you knew him sufficiently to summon him to a meeting.'
'Even if I did, do you think I would do such a thing?'

'No, of course not. Please forgive me. We'll find a way to get to him, but for Princess Bisma we would like to rely on your good offices.'

'What are you going to discuss with her? I don't want to know the crux but I must have some idea of the purpose of the meeting before I speak to her.'

After a pause, the Major said, 'I believe a proposal favouring the Princess is in the offing.'

'Do you think she will go for something like that?' Behr-e-Karam remarked surprised at the ham-fistedness of GHQ. 'And you want me to talk to her about this?'

'Not for disclosing what I've just mentioned, but only for seeking time for a meeting.'

'What would I represent myself as – your employee, your agent? Come on Major, you'd better think of a plausible link with your people if I am to appear convincing.'

Major Tariq conferred with someone on his cell phone then suggested, 'You could perhaps indicate that some friends at GHQ had enquired in passing whether an informal chat with her could be arranged. And that was all the information you had of GHQ interest.'

Bisma was surprised when Behr-e-Karam called on behalf of the GHQ but she did not question his role. Her reaction was guarded as was to be expected. She wanted time to think. She discussed the matter with Meheryar and Pir Rehbar Sharif. They suggested that she should hear what the GHQ representatives had to say. 'Abundant caution,' was what Pir sahib advised her to observe.

Deciding on a place for the meeting became a knotty issue. GHQ wanted to hold the meeting at the Deriabad station commander's office. Bisma refused. The next suggestion was Falaktaj Palace. Bisma refused. She suggested her campaign office. The GHQ representatives felt awkwad about holding a meeting in a candidate's campaign office. She then suggested that they join her at home for a cup of tea. Since that was as far as she was prepared to go, GHQ had to accept her offer, even though the prospect of negotiating delicate matters of state in a private home devoid of the requisite electronic back-up was unprecedented.

A day before the meeting, Anwar Pasha – egged on by his contacts in intelligence – turned up in Deriabad. He saw himself sitting in at the meeting as Bisma's consort. The prospect appealed to his sense of self-importance. Bisma would have none of it, pointing out he had no part in her political life or indeed in any other aspect of her life. When he reminded her that Islamic etiquette required a woman to be accompanied by a male escort when consorting with strange men, she cut him short stating that Meheryar would, as always, be there.

On the morning of the appointed day, an unannounced passenger plane bearing certain VIP negotiators landed on a remote runway at Deriabad airport.

News of the arrival got to the palace during breakfast hour.

'What are they here for?' Kulsoom asked looking up momentarily from her six egg omlette.

'How should I know,' Sartaj replied nervously.

The presence of establishment figures in Deriabad was cause for uneasiness. Unannounced visitations were particularly worrying.

Mehboob Alam Shah reached the breakfast room as they were speaking. 'Highness,' he said, 'forgive the intrusion. I came to inform you that Lieutenant General Altaf Sarfaraz and Major General Obaidullah Kaleem have landed in Deriabad this morning ...'

'We know, we know,' Sartaj said shortly. 'What are they here for? No one told me to expect them or make any special arrangements ...'

'I understand,' Mehboob Alam said, blinking rapidly, 'they are here for talks with some election candidates.'

'What,' Sartaj exclaimed, 'not to call on me? Will they be calling at the palace after their talks?'

'I don't think so, Highness. They will leave soon after the talks, I'm told.'

'This is too much,' Sartaj said. 'They come to our state, and don't have the manners to call on me.'

'I think you should send message to call on you,' Kulsoom said.

'Don't be absurd,' Sartaj said, 'best to remain silent.'

'Quite right Highness,' Mehboob Alam said, turning to go.

'Wait, Shah Sahib,' Sartaj said, filling Mehboob Alam with dread at the prospect of the so far unasked question.

'Who are they here to talk with?'

Mehboob Alam took a deep breath and said quickly, 'Princess Bisma Sultan and Ameer Bakhsh Lashari.'

'Bisma, why Bisma?' Sartaj snapped, reddening.

'How they can call on a family member without seeing the ruler first?' Kulsoom queried.

'They can do anything they like,' Mehboob Alam said. 'They are the real rulers and *our state* as we like to call it, is a part of the country they rule.'

'But what they are going to say to her?' Kulsoom asked.

'For God's sake Kulsoom, what does it matter what they say to her. Isn't it galling enough to be ignored while they go about their affairs in Deriabad?' Then as an afterthought, 'I think I'll write to the Ministry of States.'

During the course of morning, debugging experts had been over Bisma's villa with a fine toothcomb looking for concealed spying devices. That afternoon, three SUVs took the winding road to the villa. On reaching the entrance, Lieutenant General Altaf Sarfaraz stepped out of the lead SUV and trod briskly up the front steps. Meheryar and Ghulam Ali, Bisma's campaign manager, received him. Introductions were made by the station commander. Visiting negotiators included the general, ministers of the interior and defence, the station commander, Major Tariq and a stenographer.

Bisma, accompanied by Almas, awaited the visitors in the formal sitting room. The officers tipped their caps when introduced to her. The ministers greeted her with a salaam and bow of the head. They arrayed themselves in a semi-circle facing her – the stenographer poised behind the General. Meharyar, Ghulam Ali and Almas sitting on either side of Bisma.

'Tea before discussions,' Bisma suggested to get the ball rolling.

During tea Bisma felt the General's gaze sizing her up while also taking in the surroundings.

*My, my,* she thought, *a three star general just for me. Why aren't these people looking after the defence of the country instead of hobnobbing with civilians?*

'You have a beautiful home ma'am - I mean Princess,' he said in resonant tones.

'Thank you General Sahib,' she replied. *That's something. Small talk from top brass ... but he is an impressive specimen.*

And he was. Not too tall, full bodied, ruddy complexion engendered by northern climes, brush like moustache dipping slightly at the ends, and the look of a cavalier.

With the tea things gone along with Ghulam Ali and Almas, it was time to talk.

'Princess, we have imposed on your time in the national interest,' the general began, giving way to the interior minister to explain the country's problems, the objectives and achievements of the government and its important ongoing and future programmes. Forty minutes later Bisma was no wiser about the reason for the meeting.

*I suppose that's the kind of information that is trotted out to ambassadors and foreign dignitaries. Why is he telling me this?'*

'These elections,' the minister said, 'are fundamental for the democratic success of the nation.'

*More platitudes,* she mused, *but maybe we're getting closer.*

'We have noted the success of your campaign. Princess,' the minister of defence said. 'We also agree with several aspects of your agenda. We want to incorporate it in our programme.'

Taken unawares Bisma asked, 'How do you propose to do that Minister?'

'That's the reason we are here,' the interior minister said. 'We want you to consider joining the government.'

'We want you to continue with your campaign as an independent candidate,' General Sarfaraz interceded, 'but after the elections, and your success – which we will ensure – join the government by either becoming a member of the National Front, or if you prefer, by retaining your independent status.'

Bisma could not believe what she heard.

*What* a *preposterous proposition,* she thought. *I feel like laughing.* But a look in the General eye kept her from doing so.

'Well Princess, what are your views on our proposal?' the interior minister asked. 'We would of course offer you a ministerial post. You would be an asset to the government.'

Bisma glanced at Meheryar, whose face reflected her disbelief.

'I don't know what to say Minister. This is so extraordinary ... I had not expected anything like this.'

'Like what Princess?' the general said in a voice given to command. 'We have offered you a role in the future government.'

'General, if the government party is so supportive of my programme, why not wait until the election results are in before making the offer? Taking such decisions at this stage will be most awkward without even addressing the awkwardness of hijacking the citizens rights agenda.'

'That is why it was suggested that you might continue as an independent candidate, and take up the offer after the elections,' the general said fixing her with steely look.

'So the offer has been made with the intention of seeking my commitment at this particular time.'

'Precisely,' the defence minister said, 'the election is close. Pending issues must be resolved in the next few weeks.'

Sensing that the discussion was not hitting the right targets, the interior minister said, 'If the political transition is not to your liking Princess ...' a sudden gesture of impatience from General Sarfaraz stopped him.

'Please go on, Minister,' Bisma urged.

'If, as I said, joining the government is not to your liking, an ambassadorship in one of the primary interest countries will be made available.'

'But don't you realize Minister,' Bisma said in exasperation, 'that what you refer to as my programme belongs to a party, not to me. I am merely one of the members voicing the agenda. It's not something I can give to the government or anyone else. If you like the party objectives so much, you or others in power can implement them without seeking the approval of the citizens rights group or any other entity. Nothing sacrosanct about them, simply a reiteration of human rights adapted to our requirements.'

*She hasn't gone for the bait,* the general thought. *Tough character – and a dangerous one. Will stick it to the armed forces given half a chance.*

'You are significant Princess,' General Sarfaraz said evenly. 'You are the pivot of the citizens rights group. That's why the NFP wants to come to terms with you.'

'You mention the NFP, General, but what about the interests you represent?'

*Dear God,* thought Meheryar, *she is treading on thin ice ... but of course they deserve such candidness.*

'We are interested in national welfare and stand ready to help those who see things our way,' he said with a touch of menace.

'From our talks, I gather that you gentleman see me as a kind of torch bearer of the citizens rights group. And you believe that if I was to be neutralized, the group would lose steam. Do you think that the demand for citizens rights is merely a political ploy? Can't you conceive of it as a cry coming ...'

'Princess,' the general interrupted, 'no one wants another party in the field. Especially a party that has an agenda at odds with the objectives of the country's defenders. Not too much to ask, I think.'

'And what happens to the citizens rights group while you pursue your plan?'

'We will enter into an agreement, undertaking to implement their objectives which we find acceptable and to resolve the controversial ones after discussions,' the interior minister said.

Unable to restrain herself, Bisma said, 'Promises, promises. We have experienced many such situations. Despite the written word, if some of the aims conflict with the basic premise on which the rulers operate, then what goes first? And how does one sell such a convoluted deal to the voters who hold the greatest stake?'

General Sarfaraz got up with an abruptness, causing the others to jump to their feet. He seized his cap and swagger stick, and came up to Bisma.

'Thank you for your time and your hospitality, Princess. We won't be troubling you any more,' he said leaving as briskly as he had come.

*The bitch,* he thought as the SUV raced down, *is not for bending. Well, we'll see … we'll see.*

'He took it as a personal affront,' Meheryar said.

'I'm the one who is affronted,'Bisma said.'Such audacity. Suggesting that I forgo beliefs, principles and loyalties for what they offered.'

'He's obviously used to getting his way,' Meheryar said. 'So he's not likely to forget.'

'Well, we'll see … we'll see,' she murmured echoing the General.


The meeting with Ameer Bakhsh was held at the station commander's office. The negotiators included officers from the station commander's staff, the secretaries of the interior and defence ministries and a stenographer.


Faced with the formidable team around the table Ameer anticipated a grilling. Instead, it was carrot and stick session. They lauded his community welfare services (which surprised him since such matters were rarely publicised) praised his canvassing skills (which he took with a pinch of salt) and expressed wonder at his rating in the context of the polls (which he realized was what irked them). Then they put it to him – a merger of interests, either by switching over to the NFP or by joining the central order after the elections – assuming he was successful – in return for a ministry of state or a synacure public post. If the offer was refused, inquisitorial probes into the finances of local welfare services under him would be conducted by officially appointed auditors.

After hearing them out without comment, Ameer Bakhsh stood up, raised folded hands saying, 'I thank you for honouring me with your visit. I thank you for considering me worthy of your generous offer which I am not in a position to accept because that would be like supporting the old order and turning away from my commitment to Changez Khan Turkmanzai.'

He continued facing them with folded hands as he backed out of the room.

# Chapter 15

Within the final weeks of the polls the country went into a carnivalesque mode. Rallies – peopled or vehicle driven – took place in rural hamlets and urban spaces, banner bearing, flag waving processions and sloganeering public meetings were addressed countrywide by politicos. Giant billboards displayed truck art representations of Lollywoodised candidates vying for votes. Illumination from strobe, spot and digitalised sources flashed nonstop despite electricity shortage. And music … music of all genres – filmic, pop, folk, devotional, rang through in ear-splitting decibels. It was a bizarre, noisy, and garish spectacle if ever.

A container with a staging platform was arranged by Ameer Bakhsh for conveying retired Air Vice Marshal Changez Khan Turkmanzai along with some twenty of his close supporters to a public meeting at Shahryar Peoples Park. The container proceeded at the pace of a teeming crowd that accompanied it from Deriabad railway station to the town centre. Vast numbers of people kept poring into the streets. By the time the container got to the town centre a sea of heads was all that was visible.

The trip to the park was taking so long that at one stage Changez Khan thought of walking to the site but was stopped from doing so by his security team. When at last the container rolled into the park, three hours had gone by. But this was a crowd that was prepared to wait for him for as long as it took.

Before Changez Khan's appearance, Bisma's public address had been rated as a tour de force which other candidates including Maulana Sherani had failed to achieve. But now another star was in the field.

His appearance on the platform was heralded by a roar of 'Sona munda, we see you, we will hear you, we are with you.' From their vantage point in the park Sartaj's sons could feel the current that passed through the crowd. Close to the containers, Razia and her burqa clad companions felt that they were in the presence of a great leader.

Changez Khan was of medium height with the spare muscular physique of a sportsman that made him appear younger than his forty seven years. His finely etched features were livened by twinkling eyes and a clipped moustache.

He was something of a national hero for having moulded the Air Force into a first rate fighting force and also for applying extraordinary strategy to turn the tide in two air skirmishes in a war that had taken place with the neighbouring country. His subsequent retirement from service was caused by the realization that not combat skills but good governance, poverty alleviation and uprightness were the pressing needs of the nation.

Within days of his retirement he received assurances from the GHQ and the Admiralty that they would support him if he took steps to topple the government and take over the country. The religious right urged him to do just that and the business community followed suit, but an innate sensibility kept him from taking a step that would have had unpredictable consequences. Instead, he chose to enter into a memorandum of understanding with the incumbent executive for allowing the holding of free elections within a time frame – that had now come round.

His success in resolving the crisis was regarded as a national achievement of the highest order. And now here he was in Deriabad, not seeking public support as Bisma had done by promising a reformed order that would be ushered in by constitutionalism, but by calling for a revolutionary revision of the nation's mindset from laissez faire liberalism to governance by fully empowered local bodies voted in on the basis of proportional representation instead of the first past the post method of picking winners. He preferred pragmatism in defence policies. He spoke of special measures he would introduce for meeting basic needs, checking income disparity and discrimination, introducing free medicare for the poor, tackling price control and tax collection, coming down hard on nepotism, challenging national sloth by belt tightening and a work hardened regime, upholding the rule of law by a tough penal code wrought by updating the existing jumbled mass of laws.

Changez Khan stood astride on the platform with arms raised as he announced his programme to a rapt audience. 'Have you understood all that I have said?' he asked when he was done. An initial silence was followed by cries in the affirmative mingled with others that wanted him to continue speaking. To clarify the gist of his speech, he called on a member of his support team to field him questions on particular aspects of his agenda, which he then answered in terms that were comprehensible to the ordinary man. Some of the spectators came on the public address system with questions of their own. The question and answer method and the chatty follow on went down well with the crowd.

The meeting lasted till late evening. There were a few additional speeches by some members of the team which were interspersed with songs and music performed by popular entertainers.

The spectators joined in the well known songs and kept time with the beat of dance numbers. Barrow boys selling finger food and party workers distributing multicoloured pamphlets containing manifesto details peppered with satirical sketches by celebrated cartoonists, added to the festive flavour.

Towards the end Changez Khan thanked everyone for the reception he had received. 'We have had a great get together today,' he said, 'and the person responsible for this is my representative, who is also your representative, Ameer Bakhsh Lashari.'

The crowd cheered and applauded. Amidst cries of 'Ameer Bakhsh zindabad,' Ameer Bakhsh was hauled on to the platform and handed a speaker by Changez Khan. Somewhat overcome, he managed to murmur a few words about the great opportunity that had come for the country in the guise of Changez Khan's political programme. Then he called on all present to cast their votes in support of the programme to ensure its beoming national policy.

Before boarding the train, Changez Khan spent a short time at the party headquarters facing newspaper correspondents, and longer time in Allah Bakhsh's family abode.

Newsworthy events were rarely missed by Sameera. Xerxes was able to cover the highlights of Changez Khan's address. Sameera managed to clamber on the container and got round to filming and interviewing members of his team. The piece de resistance was her personal interview of Changez Khan at Allah Bakhsh's home. It was not scheduled but was arranged by Ameer Bakhsh.

Caught off guard, Changez Khan was expansive and forthcoming. He spoke of things he had not mentioned before. He was especially forthcoming about the need for a civil/military compact to promote the cause of democracy as a common objective.

'You can put forth a point of view to men in uniform, and after a while they will grasp the gist, but with civil leaders if they agree on only one thing, it is to pursue individual agendas.'

But by making room for the military in this scheme will be a denial of the democratic norm,' Sameera commented.

'Not at all,' Changez Khan said, 'it is the success of a scheme that counts, not who brings it about.'

'But why the armed forces?'

'Can you trust our civil leaders in totality? They are so far removed from democracy. Individual interests and party loyalty come first and official power is used to promote them.'

'And how do you see the role of the military in this?'

'It is the only institution that civil leaders are mindful of in preference to the electorate.'

It will hold them to democratic practice. It will push and cajole and prompt. In the final analysis it will warn. It will remain focused on two objectives, the country's survival and its survival as a democracy.'

An evening at the Royal Daryadar Hunting Lodge topped off Sameera's visit. Her unit would return to base the following morning. Meheryar had invited them for dinner.

'I shall miss this fairytale atmosphere when I am back in the brutal city,' Sameera said.

'Come back and visit us whenever.' Meheryar remarked.

'Perhaps on election day. Someone has to cover that.'

'It's been a great experience for us, Prince,' Xerxes said. 'Until I got here, I could not have imagined a place like Deraiabad. Apart from the history, the monuments and the natural beauty, the people are unlike any other.'

'The coverage has been unbelievable,' Sameera said.

'It has probably been as eventful elsewhere too,' Meheryar said.

'Not so, Prince,' Xerxes said. 'Here we have been exposed to the major pronouncements of the next leaders of the country, your sister, Princess Bisma, Tehreek's Ameer Bakhsh and the man himself, Changez Khan.'

'We've seen campaigning of the highest order,' Sameera said.

During the week of their stay in Deriabad, clips of items of coverage appeared daily on the Tasveer-e-Watan.

Two days after their return, several networks, aired a marathon presentation on the Deriabad campaign prepared by Sameera much to the annoyance of Kulsoom.

The TV coverage gave a filip to the election fervour in Deriabad. A holiday atmosphere seemed to take over. No one was interested in their working responsibilities. School children marched up and down the streets waving flags and banners. The teaching staff busied themselves setting up the procedural requirements for the polling. The streets teamed with processions and rallies and sales of *pakoras, samosas* and *chaat*. Music blared into the night while the town kept awake.

The PBX telephone at Deriabad House rang several times. The private secretary to Pir Sahib Rehbar Sharif was calling to check if Princess Bisma Sultan would need a car for getting to a meeting of the governing body of the citizens rights group at Pir Sahib's residence. It was explained that the Princess would be using her own transport.

Bisma, accompanied by Meheryar had arrived that morning, to the great relief of Ninette and the twins who had felt somewhat ostracized after the Paris incident.

'Mama sends her love to all of you,' Bisma said handing out Rani Satrangi's gifts. 'She says, you're to forget all that has happened and face Sartaj Bhaijan as if explanations were unnecessary.'

'Everyone knows you're not to blame for the accident.'

'That's very reassuring,' Ninette said, 'and I'm grateful to Rani Sahib. Let's face it though, I could have been more firm and kept us out of that crazy episode.'

'You were left with no option, Mummy,' Rabby said,

'A ridiculous position to be in … I should have known better.'

'Come on Lady N,' Meheryar said, 'no one doubts your intentions or your loyalty to the family. It's an unfortunate occurrence that could've happened to anyone.'

'Yes, but let's not overlook the consequences … the girls' lives were at risk, and … Sadie's engagement was in jeopardy … and the newspaper aspersions …'

'You don't want to know about the aspersions and innuendos I have been getting since I announced my candidature,' Bisma said. 'We learn to live with it. The Umranis have broad shoulders and we've overcome greater obstacles. This is no more than a social slur, and it'll fade away in time.'

'I suppose so,' Ninette said, still pursued by doubt.

'Anyway you'll have to face the lions at Sadie's wedding in Deriabad next month.'

Pir Sahib Rehbar Sharif lived in a suburb of the port city that had been a hub for gracious living of Hindu merchants in colonial times. The once wide and well spread roads running between rows of looming mansions were now taken over by the squatting syndrome which pervaded the bazaars and low end commercial areas of the city. It was crowded with barrows laden with bric a brac, baskets of edibles, makeshift stalls and *khokas* or *dhabas* frying spicy concoctions, tail flicking donkey and camel cart haulers, and ubiquitous beggars.

The car driving Bisma and Meheryar had to weave its way through these impediments to get to Pir Sahib's home. The houses they passed were crumbling art deco mansions built in large compounds with plenty of old trees and gardens that had gone to seed. Most of them were subdivided into separate living quarters for owners and tenants. Others housed cottage industries, tailoring outfits or repairers of electronic goods or vehicles.

A few old-timers like Pir Sahib had preserved the genteel tradition recalling erstwhile sumptuousness.

'It's a never ending struggle to keep the tide outside these walls from swamping our little island,' Pir Sahib complained.

Bisma was pleased at seeing Pir Sahib. His roly-poly gnome like appearance reminded her of a hobbit.

'In here it's like a time capsule,' she said.

'You wouldn't say so if the building mafia that's taken over the city had got here. Thank God it has been kept away – for the time being – by our construction regulations. Otherwise there would have been low cost high rises going up on every other plot dwarfing the few remaining houses.

'A city brimming with shabby apartment chawls,' Meheryar said sadly.

'Planning, aesthetics, history, leisure, all gone by the board for profit,' Pir Sahib remarked.

'Take heart, Pir Sahib. It's for tackling such abuses that we've come together,' Bisma said reassuringly.

'I leave you with your seven dwarves,' Meheryar murmured quietly to Bisma before slipping out to attend to business matters.

Bisma's appearance at the meeting, was greeted by muted applause led by co-founder Altamash Arbab whose leanness was in marked contrast to Pir Sahib's rotundity.

Her questioning look on the applause drew a response from the third founder, Dr. Jasmin Jalal, 'The reports about your campaign are most heartening. The national press has cited your objectives in inverted commas, as striking just the right chord for a programme of national revival. We couldn't have asked for anything better for all our candidates' chances.'

She went on to introduce new members to Bisma who was pleasantly surprised to note that one of them was Mr. Aminuddin, Hussain's father and Sadie's prospective father-in-law.

Many of those standing for election got an opportunity to discuss campaigning issues. All reported on having to face the hostility of the National Front election machine backed by the establishment. General strategy for dealing with these and other exigencies was mooted and countermeasures suggested. A decision by consensus was taken on delaying the group's registration as a political party until after the elections. For the time being candidates were advised to contest the election as independent entities. Other decisions dealt with the formal drafting of the objectives, and the agenda of the group and the need for a budget. The meeting continued till late evening

'The last few weeks have been quite eventful.' Canny Kamran announced in the vault.

'Harrumph!' uttered the Eldest Elder.

'Two of our descendants are slogging it out in the national election, both Steadfast Shahryar's children. His daughter Bisma is being opposed tooth and nail by that moron passing for the nawab.'

'Don't be disrespectful about the head of the family,' said Fussy Farhad.

'Uneasy lies the head ... dee da daa,' sang Artful Arbab.

'You're an irreverent bunch of corpses,' Fussy Farhad said. 'You have all been rulers in days gone by and now that you're not, you think nothing of disparaging those who have taken your place.'

'Come, come,' Greybeard said, 'this is not something we should be quarrelling about.'

'I'd call it jealousy,' Fussy Fahad said. 'They're just envious that they're down here, and their successors are now ruling the roost.'

'Envious of that nincompoop Sartaj!' Canny Kamran said, 'He doesn't know his elbow from his...'

'Now, now, there is no need to use scurrilous language,' Eldest Elder said, 'I think we are expected to be gentlemen of the grave. We were nawabs once and trustees of a great heritage.'

'Well, we're not that now, are we?' Grumbles said. 'Dead is dead, and that's what we are.'

'It's difficult not be interested in what goes on above,' Curioso said.

'Why?' Grumbles asked. 'We've left that behind. Makes no difference to us. Wise corpses focus on their future.'

'For the ultimate pay off eh,' Canny Kamran remarked.

'Don't be coarse,' Grumbles replied.

'The standard of family behaviour falls with each generation,' Fussy Farhad said.

'What is that supposed to mean?' Artful Arbab asked.

'They aren't above the masses any more, setting standards for all to follow – as royalty is meant to do. They're part of the crowd now – doing what the hoi polloi does except for being better dressed and in grand surroundings.'

'Things have changed with the new democratic order,' Canny Kamran said.

'If that's what the democratic order brings about then we are best out of it,' Fussy Farhad said.

'Once upon a time,' Grumbles said, 'there was God, then the British crown, then the *riyasat* and country. Nowadays it's the rabble leading eunuchs like Sartaj by the short and curly.'

The graves shook with laughter.

'Consider what the present lot is up to,' Fussy Farhad said guffawing. 'There's Sartaj with his bottom heavy wife perched like Scrooge on top of the pile moaning and groaning about expenses. Then we have Bisma traipsing around without that faggot of a husband behaving for all the world like the Rani of Jhansi on campaign, except that it's not a battle she's facing but an election for representing the sweaty multitude whose votes she courts by speechifying in public parks.'

'Let's not overlook that French pastry Sharyar brought home,' Curioso said.

'How can one overlook her after she disgraced the family in Paris … Dowager Begum indeed!' Grumbles said.

'The ignominy of an Umrani nawab's daughter being engaged to a common trader from a minority community.' Curioso added.

'Yes of course, Fussy Farhad said. 'She has turned that pair of princesses into parlour maids or something worse. They flit around the port city like Hefner's bunnies wagging their bobbed tails.'

'I wonder how many of you know that a prince of the household has become a government stooge,' Curioso said.

'That Behr-e-Karam always was a bit of a Mir Jaffar,' Greybeard said. 'I have had doubts about his pedigree for long.'

'Why don't their mothers stop them from crossing lines royals are meant to observe?' Arful Arbab said. 'One would assume they knew better.'

'All over the hill now, I'm afraid,' Canny Kamran said.'Anyway who listens to them. That guttersnipe wife of Sartaj always challenges Badshah Begum. Rani Satrangi is tough but Bisma's marriage failed anyway. Couldn't take the gay scene. Nothing wrong with it. Some of us have tumbled the odd boy in our time.'

'Speak for yourself',snapped Fussy Farhad.

'Then there's the Frenchie,' Canny Kamran continued. 'What a collection Shahryar left behind. It's a mercy that he is still asleep and can't hear what we're saying.'

A momentary stirring in Shahryar's grave caused jitters in several graves.

'What a shame. Royalty taken over by the commonplace. Who foresaw that the House of Umran would fall so low.' Fussy Farhad said.

'Ready for oblivion,' Grumbles intoned.

# Chapter 16

Sadie's wedding celebrated with aplomb in Deriabad and the Port City, brought the Umranis together just before the polls.

The festive spirit carried on morphing into pre-election fever. Governmental agencies with stakes in the polls had a set up their bases in Deriabad. All was in readiness.

Since the Deriabad constituencies were not too large or unwieldy, the polls were expected to be over by sundown.

On election morning, queues of voters were lined up in cordoned off areas surrounding the polling stations. Everything seemed in order. Representatives of the Election Commission and NAB officers helped locate names and numbers of incumbents from voters lists and guided them on the correct voting procedure.

Early signs of irregularity occurred when Tehreek-i-Awam workers objected to voters lists bearing dummy names. On checking, it was apparent that several names were missing although voting slips had been issued in favour of some of the missing names and were being cast in ballot boxes.

The Election Commission officials took note of these incidents, and removed such boxes after sealing them. Several National Front workers raised objection to the removal of those boxes. They claimed that valid votes cast in favour of their candidates would be nullified by such arbitrariness.

At another polling booth the citizens rights group came upon fingerprint stamping favouring King's party candidates proceeding briskly on blank voter slips. The votes were rapidly checked and only the verified ones were cast in the ballot boxes since the time remaining for the election process was drawing to an end.

Workers of the citizens right groups and of Tehreek-e-Awam raised objections at polling stations where new irregularities kept happening. Some of the altercations became heated, resulting in skirmishes.

The most violent incidents occurred at the polling stations in the constituencies Bisma stood for. Groups of men and women tried to take over the ground spaces around the ballot boxes by edging out the polling staff. This led to grappling and fisticuffs. Citizens groups workers were able to get at the disruptionists. There were plenty of black eyes, bloody noses and some broken bones. Ultimately the rangers were able to nab the troublemakers – including women – for the police lock-up.

By the evening most of the spectators had left the campaign area, chastened and disillusioned.

Despite the many objections to the conduct of the polls, Deriabad, like the rest of the country, took its losses and wins in its stride. The attempt to besmear Bisma for which the NFP had set aside a large budget, came to naught. Deriabad citizens were not ready to buy into Bisma's shortcomings.

The results of the election came as eye-openers for the public. Bisma won two of her constituencies, FA 148 and FA 150 with sweeping majorities. She lost FA 153 to Ameer Bakhsh by a narrow margin. The National Front and other parties were reduced to a nominal holding of seats.

'It's about time,' Ghulam Ali said, 'that the tide turned to show us the underside of the water.'

The Deriabad result was not confined to the state. The electoral experience was repeated on a countrywide basis. The assessments of the governmental agencies involved in political management of national affairs had been wrong. They required considerable reworking. They were forced to assimilate the new realities and try to make sense of emerging viable associations. Arduous replanning had to be done to bring about new alignments which would meet their long term plan for maintaining national control.

Lieutenant General Altaf Sarfaraz had no working experience with AVM Changez Khan Turkmanzai, although he had been an important part of the state apparatus that dealt with the country's defence. General Altaf resented having to negotiate with the AVM, as he looked upon the army as the superior force. He had no option except to twist his rosary in knots when an official spokesman addressed the nation announcing that the election was over. The mandate had been won by the AVM. It was a landslide victory. The numbers cited were cheered loud and long.

When the national network caught up with the AVM, his approach was singular. He acknowledged the electioneering services conducted by the rangers. He congratulated them on facilitating a free election according to the memorandum of understanding he had arrived at with the incumbent power brokers before the elections.

He expounded on the need for governance by fully empowered local bodies elected by proportional representation. He emphasised the enforcement of the rule of law by a revised tough penal code, hard work and belt tightening. He emphasized that he would prefer the government to be run as a coalition with the citizens rights group. He also emphasised the need for a pragmatic approach on defence matters.

The fallout was quite different from the prepared scenario. The fake voter lists did not work, the missing voters were not forthcoming, the lists of dummy fingerprints fell by the wayside.

The government agencies that had worked for a favourable result seemed forlorn. They busied themselves with assimilating their electoral paraphernalia, before returning to the capital. Townsfolk went about giving vent to their feelings. The roads in and out of town were clogged with all manner of vehicles.

The atmosphere at the palace was somewhat stifling. Sartaj had locked himself in with his stamp collection. Kulsoom nibbled from the bowls of finger food scattered about. The boys kept busy with the latest reports coming in.

At Allah Bakhsh's home in Pattanwala, village folk and locals called to express their pleasure at Ameer Bakhsh's success. It was a brand new experience for them – not only having one of their kind elected but also appointed as the area representative in the National Assembly. There were celebration. Young people sang and danced to the beat of the *dholak* late into the night.

The dust had barely begun to settle on the aftermath of the elections, before the power brokers met and conferred. They admitted that the AVM had a colossal majority and if linked with the citizens group, the outcome would be overwhelming. Any success for spoilers was not going to be attained by numbers. The answer lay in low skirmishes, bush fires started at the provincial level, official incompetence blown sky high, financial irregularities aired, scandal mongering, a hostile press, buying influence. All such measures were to be orchestrated into an anti-government campaign for loosening the grip encircling it.

Meanwhile the various political parties with winning candidates got busy laying the groundwork for their parliamentary strategies. The Tehreek-e-Awam held post- electoral meetings at its headquarters in the capital. The citizens group met at the port city. Both parties were aware that the Tehreek wanted to enter into a coalition with the citizens group. Some of the committee members of the citizens group were not keen on joining the Tehreek. They felt their significance would be muted by the large number of seats taken by the Tehreek in the National Assembly.

Pir Sahib of Rehbar Sharif did not comment on the proposed coalition, but Dr. Jasmin Jaleel and Altamash Arbab were not in favour of it. Pir Sahib suggested that all the committee members should get an opportunity to present their views on the proposal, after which a vote could be taken.

When it came to Bisma's turn, she supported the idea of the coalition. She alluded to the large lead the Tehreek had over others in the popular vote, indicating their hold on the voters. She was of the view that the Tehreek sought the coalition because of the political programme announced by the citizens rights group.

She felt that was their strength and that they could promote it with some success in the new government. There was also nothing in the Tehreek's policies that her party was averse to.

Being in the opposition, they would be able to give voice to their agenda in the House, but takers would be hard to find, as the political strength of the Tehreek was unlikely to diminish until at least the midterm of its mandate. 'We could always leave the coalition if things did not work out,' she concluded.

The committee voted in favour of the coalition, accepting the Tehreek's offer. In the new dispensation announced a few days later, Bisma was given the ministerial portfolio of local affairs along with a department for citizens' welfare.

After the oath-taking ceremony of the new members at a joint session of the National Assembly and the Senate a reception was held for the new entrants. AVM Changez Khan in the role of the Primeminister was swamped by newsmen anxious to pick up his first words. Other MNAs were also sought out. Among the lady MNAs, Bisma was probably the most sought after by the press. She answered most of the questions in even tones touching upon aspects of the citizens group policies that coincided with the Tehreek's objectives.

Ameer Bakhsh Lashari, virtually unknown at that gathering stood out amidst the swirling crowd. Immaculate in white salwar kameez, white waistcoat and a light turban, he declined the refreshments offered, preferring to observe other guests with dark, unblinking eyes. His bearded handsomeness and clearly ringing voice were not overlooked by some at the oath-taking.

Despite his protestations, Ameer Bakhsh was appointed minister for water resources and housing. He doubted his capability and work experience in assuming such important responsibilities, but the AVM overrode his reservations, sensing – intuitively – that Ameer Bakhsh had sufficient know-how required for the task.

Following the reception, the AVM had invited the cabinet to his home for dinner.

'It's a coming together evening,' he said, 'so that you people get to know each other. After all we will be working as a team to achieve declared objectives, so it is a good time to check each other out. All policy matters will have equal significance irrespective of whether they emanate from the Tehreek-e-Awam or the citizens group. Once adopted the policy would be recognized as a government backed move.' He made it a point to say a few words about each person as he went around the room.

Anwar Pasha was keen for Bisma to stay at his home, and called her attention to the comments that would arise if she stayed elsewhere. Bisma was unmoved. She did not want to have anything to do with him, subconsciously wanting all to know about it.

She organised her living arrangements at the capital with swift efficiency at the MNA lodge. She was attended by a maid who could cook and a driver. Her apartment could accommodate three house guests. Her mornings were spent at the Assembly. In the afternoons she presided over her ministries. Lunch was at the Assembly eatery, or with a friend. Evenings meals were spent at home unless she was invited out. Most of her evenings were spent in ministerial work, or catching up on world affairs and reading.

Bisma and Ameer Bakhsh had their first face to face encounter in the lift of the lodge in which they were billeted. He raised his hand in a salaam and she responded. She got out at the second floor leaving a trace of jasmine in the lift, and he carried on till the fourth floor.

Ameer Bakhsh was on another plane. Often he felt like a fish out of water, or a vagrant who has hopped up many steps to emerge in a world to which he did not belong. On seeing the accommodation available in the apartment, he called his father and asked him to send three of his brothers to live with him.

'I'll get a job for the older one, and he can take care of the flat and food. As for other two, I'll get them into a good school.'

'What about Razia?' Allah Bakhsh asked.

'She can come on a visit when I say so, but this is not a place where a peasant woman with small children can live.'

'How does it feel Ameer Bakhsh … now that you have achieved the grand future you used to argue about?'

Ameer Bakhsh fell silent, then said, 'Abbaji, I'm nervous …but the freedom has gone … in its place there's a great new responsibility.'

Most of the day was spent at the Assembly, attending sessions regularly or learning House business, but come afternoon he was eager to get to the ministries to absorb what he needed to know to attain competence in his role.

When not working he was in the library, or on long walks getting to know his way round the capital. He soon learned how to deal with the questions raised during question hour. When it came to addressing the House on policy, he prepared his statements in advance. He even developed the skill of blunting off-the-cuff remarks with ripostes. With the growth of confidence and his habit of looking a person in the eye, the members of House came to regard him as a person to be taken seriously – not one to be gulled by political doubletalk.

'You are unlikely to become a peacock by mingling with them,' Razia had taunted Ameer Bakhsh when he was preparing to leave for the capital.

'Is that what you think I want to be?' he had asked.

'No, because I know you as a decent man leading a straight-forward life but this is different. They say you will be made a minister. *Sona munda* has great faith in you. You'll be working with the topmost people in the country. Since you will gain importance, I'm just reminding you of the old saying.'

He thought of Razia's comments on one of his walks. He had a job trying to dodge the security guards when he took his walks. It was especially irritating when he wanted to be alone to focus on his thoughts.

Aiming to gain their confidence he said, 'I am just like you. No one will take me for a minister.'

'Even so, sir,' one of them said, 'we are meant to keep you safe at all times. If the security chief gets to know of your walks without an escort, we will lose our jobs.'

'Very well,' he said, 'I don't want you to lose your jobs on my account, so follow me but please keep a safe distance between us. I also want you to change into your everyday wear when you're with me, otherwise the people we come across will tie you in with me.'

*I am more like them than the people I work with*, was what struck him while walking through a wooden glade alive with wild flowers. *I've seen the MNAs at close quarters. Apart from their grand titles like nawab, sardar, pir, sahibzada, there is nothing special about them. Why would I want to be like them? I, the peasant Ameer Bakhsh from Pattanwala, Deriabad who has been singled out to do a job, I am still learning about. When I have learned enough, I will do the job God-willing, and return to my home as peasant Ameer Bakhsh.*

A path forded over a bubbling brook and went on to join a highway running parallel to the glade. Ameer Bakhsh got on to the highway for the walk back home. The guards were not far behind. A SUV drove past him, then stopped a few minutes later. The curly grey head of Jamote Wali Mohammad, a Tehreek-e-Awam MNA, appeared at a window. He called out to Ameer Bakhsh,

'Lashari sahib why are you walking. We can give you a lift back to the city. I have Makhdum Safdar Ali Jamote with me. From the SUV interior Makhdum greeted Amir Bakhsh. Drawing guns, the guards rushed to the SUV when they saw Ameer Bakhsh engaged with the car inhabitants.

'Ho ho, what are they? Your private army.'

'Just some guards appointed to escort me when I venture outdoors … It's all right chaps,' he said in colloquial tongue, 'these are friends from the National Assembly.'

'Out for your evening stroll were you. Join us for the return journey and we can chat about matters of interest.'

Ameer Bakhsh was reluctant to do so, pointing to his guards to indicate that SUV may not accommodate all.

'Let them follow on foot,' said the booming voice of Makhdum Safdar. It left Ameer Bakhsh with little option except to climb in next to the driver. As the SUV drove off, Jamote remarked, 'The Assembly has started off well … let's hope it continues this way.'

'Insha'Allah,' Ameer Bakhsh retorted.

'No fun so far,' Makhdum Safdar remarked, 'no heated arguments, accusations flung about, filibustering …'

'Makhdum Sahib,' Ameer Bakhsh said, 'isn't that the way a civilized national forum should be conducted?'

'I mean everyone seems to be in general agreement. The only questions raised have been about the capability of some office holders.'

'Don't worry Makhdum Sahib. We have a history of parliamentary battles. You'll see them erupt soon enough,' Jamote Wali Mohammad said.

'That's a gloomy forecast,' Ameer Bakhsh said.

'Well let's talk of other matters that are of common interest,' Makhdum Safdar said.

'Yes indeed,' Jamote said looking directly at Ameer Baksh, 'I hear something is afoot regarding an important legislative programme.'

'Yes, I've heard that too,' Makhdum said.

'I can't speak for the other ministries, but we are involved in progressive schemes.' Ameer Bakhsh said.

'Do give us an idea of what kind of moves are planned and in what priority?'

'Makhdum Sahib, you know parliamentary etiquette. How can a member talk about legislative measures that have not been introduced in the Assembly?'

'We're not seeking an itemized account of legislation proposed … only the departments that will be affected by these important measures,' Jamote said, 'what for instance is proposed for education, agriculture, bilateral trade, law and order, housing …'

The reference to housing drew a long breath from the Makhdum.

'Jamote sahib, I am not in a position to discuss anything on the subjects mentioned. Most of them do not concern me.'

'Oh yes, housing does.'

'I hear there is a grand plan to develop major housing projects for low income groups.'

By this time they had come near a traffic signal which was close to the parliamentary lodges. Ameer Bakhsh thanked Jamote and Makhdum hastily and got out of the SUV.

# Chapter 17

There was indeed something afoot. At the next cabinet meeting, on the conclusion of discussion on the agenda, Bisma got up on a point of order and sought the AVM's permission to address the cabinet.

She raised an issue which cut across pending policy matters. 'A government's first priority is the administration of the country for the betterment of its citizens in accordance with progressive objectives. Yet there are times when using ad hoc approaches gets you positive results.'

'Are you suggesting that in such situations long term consequences should be ignored or that the scheduling of our workload should be done on a day to day basis?' asked a gruff voice.

'Minister,' she responded, 'I was not suggesting that anything be done off-handedly, but drawing attention to the circumstances in which we work and the limited time available for resolving exigencies.'

'What is the purpose of this talk?' asked Zarina Adamkhail Minister for Home Affairs, and a formidable presence in the Assembly.

'Begum Sahib,' Bisma said, 'we are at the threshold of a new governance. We have many advantages: a skilled team of members "unlike the past beleagured six cabinets" says the New York Business Recorder. We can therefore achieve declared targets.'

Someone clapped faintly, prompting others to tap the table.

'Princess,' the AVM said. 'I applaud your faith in our team, but where do we go from here?'

'I apologise PM for the digression but a brief introduction will explain my purpose better.'

'Very well, let's hear what you have to say.'

'For the first time in the last thirty five years of our nationhood, there is a harmonious tone. After decades of misgovernance a new sanity seems to be drawing all of us closer on objectives. The agenda of the Tehreek and the agenda of our group and the PMs speech to the cabinet, have the same resonance. Both reflect a common sense understanding of our problems. If we focus our attention on primary objectives, we will be successful. Yet we need to have consensus on priorities'.

'So how do you propose to achieve consensus on primary objectives?' asked a younger member.

'I suggest that on the basis of the objectives set out in the Tehrik's agenda, all department heads should prepare a comprehensive memorandum of their departmental aims, proposed policies and targets. The completed memoranda should be studied by every cabinet member and ranked A, B or C, taking into account the merits, policy implications and importance of priorities. After all the memoranda have been rated, a review of the scores will determine which memorandum receives the highest number of As, Bs and Cs. In this way we will have a consensus on the top rankers.'

'Are we supposed to play parlour games in the cabinet?' asked an irate member.

'Let the lady finish her presentation,' the Minister of Commerce cut in.

'This additional work should be dealt with on a priority basis by devising ways and means to attend to it along with our regular workload.'

'You're asking for a cabinet of supermen and women,' said Begum Zarina.

Bisma's quip that that was what 'some of us had claimed to be when canvassing' drew a round of laughter.

On the date fixed for the review of the ratings, the cabinet members trooped in, some grumbling about the meaningless exercises Bisma had prevailed on the AVM to agree to. Others wondering what hold she had on the AVM.

All the ratings were collected and separated department-wise. Ratings for declared objectives were then aggregated by an accountant from the Ministry of Finance, and the total number of As Bs and Cs scored by each objective were written on a score board.

The highest scorer of As was National Defence. The second choice was the Alleviation of Poverty. There was a hushed silence while the members took in the numbers—which was broken by the AVM, 'Now at least we know the significance of the matters we are dealing with.'

The AVM took the matter a step further by appointing committees which would head task forces set up to devise, deal with and implement programmes that required priority handling.

'Defence,' said the AVM has special arrangements and plans which we cannot better, so it's best left to its ways and means ... poverty alleviation however, is very much our responsibility so we have to deal with that.'

The committee set up for poverty alleviation included Bisma, Ameer Bakhsh, Begum Zarina and some others. It met twice a week to identify and provide for the major problems in poverty alleviation.

Bisma found Ameer Bakhsh capable and innovative. He completed assignments on statistics and prepared reports on papers sent by foreign consultants promptly. He was also useful as a sounding board and often rounded off a topic in discussion.

Initially, he had been hesitant to work with her, but learned to overcome his reservation on account of compatibility of views. Even Begum Zarina and her colleagues came to recognise Bisma's pivotal role in their programme.

'To identify all the facets of poverty is a Herculean task, so let us focus on the addressing the leading causes,' suggested a bearded member.

'That's a good idea,' Begum Zarina said.

'Yes,' Ameer Bakhsh agreed, 'and it can be done fairly swiftly.'

The leading causes were readily identifiable as: lack of education, unemployment, absence of essential health facilities, unrestricted birth rate, overpopulation and homelessness.

'We will not be able to address all of these,' Bisma said, 'so let us put our heads together and locate a common cause. Finding primary causes is usually a step to finding a solution.'

'It would help if attending to one cause would help eradicate the need altogether,' Ameer Bakhsh said.

'Pipe dream, my boy,' said Begum Zarina.

'Many of the poverty causes are departmental subjects. Education, for instance has its own ministry, as do unemployment, health, birth control and population,'said the bearded member.

'What about homelessness?' Ameer Bakhsh queried.

'Well, what of it?' asked another.

'In the rural areas, homelessness is a major cause of poverty, because nothing belongs to the homeless.' Ameer Bakhsh said.

'Why just the rural areas, if you drive around certain parts of town,' Begum Zarina said, 'you will see the homeless sleeping on pavements, spilling over on to the roads with their children clinging to them, Mumbai style.'

'So homelessness may be a cause in itself. How do we set about addressing it?'

'The state will have to make homes for the homeless.'

'The raw materials for building a home include land,' said Ameer Bakhsh, 'plus building material, labour and other essentials.'

'How does a cash strapped government raise the funds for this?'

'Aid, grants and diversion of funds,' said the accountant, 'which are easier said than done.'

Bisma who had been deep in thought, spoke out,'I would like to share the outline of a plan with you which I have been mulling over for a while ... I also expect you to participate.'

'Land,' she said at length, 'is the base. Since most of the land belongs to the state, this can be made available without cost. After identification and marking out, it should be plotted and a model house – designed by our architects – should be constructed on it. Stereotypes of the house made up of prefabricated sections from China or Japan – should be built in rows, and thus you will have set up a mass housing community.

'Now comes the difficult part. The homeless families – mind you, not individuals – but families: father, mother, children – living in the vicinity of the building site have to be scanned at a centre set up to separate the deserving from the non-deservers. After allocation of homes to the deserving, titles to the homes will be registered. The title holder to the houses will be the state and the allottee. He will have to pay a designated sum as monthly instalment to the state. He will not have the right to alter the house structurally. He will have twenty five years more or less to make full payment. Meanwhile he will not have the authority to sell, mortgage or dispose of the house. If he does so, he will lose the house. Should be die before his term is over, the wife and sons will step into his shoes.

Such schemes should be adopted on a countrywide basis. Despite that we will not be able to house all the homeless, but if it becomes a national project then succeeding governments will be required to follow it and self-sustaining townships will develop.'

She sat back finally placing her hands under her chin.

'Bisma,' Begum Zarina asked, 'did you plan all that?'

'No way,' Bisma said, 'Mr. Ameer Bakhsh, the accountant, the Minister for Housing and the population consultants, are all part of this.'

'Well it sounds doable, but where are you going find the land?'

'Begum Sahib,' Ameer Bakhsh said, 'the country has no dearth of land. The rural areas are teeming with cultivated and hundreds of acres of uncultivated state owned land, but the largest land holdings are in and around the cities. Look around, there are so many empty or cordoned of plots with nothing on them.'

A summation of the findings of the committee had to be submitted to the cabinet.

Preparation of the report was a major undertaking. The presentation was six hours long. Further data was required for the AVM's evaluation. He also sought Bisma's views and took into account the report each member of the Poverty Alleviation (PA) team had drawn up.

On Friday after the noon prayers, the AVM addressed the cabinet, directing several remarks at the PA committee.

'You are suggesting that a new innovative policy be included in this government's five year plan. You have indeed done a great deal of work in putting together a mammoth report which certain cabinet members, foreign consultants and aid agencies have reviewed. It is good work and it is something that should be done, so I am going to announce it to the House and Senate before I address the press.'

The newspapers soon took up the refrain using their own language to describe the project. Some gave it a slant indicating that the government would be allotting choice lands for poor housing colonies. Word spread rapidly causing jitters amongst property dealers. Far right newspapers supported by the feudal lobby were very critical and published their own figures and summations to discredit the project. Nevertheless, it was government policy now and a team designated as the Poverty Alleviation Committee (PAC) headed by Bisma as CEO with Ameer Bakhsh as Co-Director was appointed to execute it. Both had to resign from their previously held ministries, but continued to retain ministerial status.

The matter was discussed in the Assembly and several motions were raised. The land lobby argued long and hard about government dishonesty in land selection, preferential locations, propagandising the homeless, applying a variable yard stick for allotments, and the extent of foreign and local cost commitments.

The AVM explained that giving homeless people a stake in land was essential for creating self-reliance and it gave them added incentive for earning a livelihood, for maintaining an ongoing household and also for ultimately getting ownership. 'Why can't you see it as a national responsibility that future governments will carry on?'

Despite popular support for the scheme in the Assembly, the loudest clamour came from a clutch of influential malcontents. Opinion makers countrywide took their time coming to grips with the project. Many found merit in it, the few who did not were close to the naysayers.

The move had roused the country more then expected. The dissidents were powerful persons: major landowners, religious authorities, government officials who had built their homes or business premises on government land, others – and there were many – who had taken illegal possession of land, altered land registration records and used it for cultivation if it was agricultural, or for putting up shopping malls and high rise buildings if it was urban.

Hardened activists and policy making interventionists opposed to the project called on their allies in government, armed forces, security agencies, clerical circles, the press and even in foreign agencies, seeking ways and means, to defeat the government's plans.

Meanwhile the PA unit, was kept busy devising practical and purposeful means to launch the programme. The AVM had selected a site close to an industrial area in a major city for the first settlement.

At the conclusion of the nationally publicised thirty day notice for unauthorised occupants to leave the land, the bulldozers moved in, tearing down, demolishing and levelling the land. Squatters deprived of their holdings stood along the boundaries of the land protesting and clamouring about the unjustness of the move. Some tried to enter the land but were forced back by armed rangers.

A rally of townsfolk in trucks and idle labourers assembled in no time. Chanting anti-government slogans, it circled the land then set off for the town centre to rouse more protesters. The local merchants guild who supported the programme – along with hundreds of madrassah students, hospital staff, teachers and housewives – had arranged a counter-rally which faced the protestors head on. The rangers were called in to quell ensuing riots and check the property damage. TV and news media had a field day, but sources that had done true pictorial coverage of the affected land before and after clearance, revealed the truth.

In the following week work had started, signalled by the arrival of drilling and boring equipment, bulldozers, concrete mixers and cranes. A section of the land was reserved for storage of crates of building parts, that kept arriving by sea or overland.

A temporary registration centre had been set up near the site. Queues of poor families lined up for evaluation of their entitlement for inclusion in the allotment.

'I've never seen such an effort before in this country,' said a foreman to a labour supervisor.

'That's because the top man wants it done speedily.'

'It may be a way to silence his critics.'

'No, I think it's more than that. It feels that he is on some kind of mission.'

On the day scheduled for the foundation laying, the law and order teams kept a firm check on the crowds. A red carpeted dais with media equipment and rows of chairs under shamianas had been set up. Guests included representatives of the government, armed forces, MNAs, eminent civilians, businessmen and the corps diplomatic. A special row was earmarked for the ambassadors of countries participating in the project and representatives of donor bodies.

The programme started with a recitation of a Quranic passage, followed by a brief welcome address by the Foreign Secretary. The AVM's speech mentioned the genesis of the project, and the national and international coordination involved to put it together. He identified and thanked the countries and agencies that had provided assistance. At the end of his speech, a foundation stone of black granite with gold lettering – was gently eased into the space arranged for it to the strains of the national anthem.

When it was her turn – as CEO of PAC and minister – to speak, in well modulated tones, Bisma explained relevant aspects of the programme from conceptualisation to home allotment. A visual presentation of how the project was expected to work, followed. A medley of the national anthems of the concerned countries played by the police band wound up the event.

# Chapter 18

On the death anniversary of the ruler, Ninette and Rabby returned to Deriabad. The anniversary formalities were held at the royal tombs. Since this was traditionally a male function, the Umrani ladies did not participate.

It was initiated by a recitation from the Quran followed by a speech in praise of the ruler by a celebrity scholar. A brief session of poetry eulogising the ruler preceded an open to all lunch, laid out under shamianas spread out for a large crowd. For the next two days Qawwalis were performed, interspersed with prayers, recitations and meals.

Within the palace precincts, the begums held a lunch for women. The event concluded when the princes led by Nawab Sartaj laid wreaths on the ruler's grave and prayed.

The next day Ninette and Rabby went to the royal tombs, where Ninette held a private tete a tete with the ruler between sobs. After they left the custodian held up his hands remarking, 'How rarely they come, but at least they do come when it matters.'

The vaulted chamber was all astir.

'It was befitting of them to come,' said Greybeard, 'it felt good to sense their presence.'

'Befitting!' said Grumbles, 'it suited them to come now.'

'You have become a real curmudgeon. When you were in the world didn't you go where you wanted to and do the things you wanted to? Well, they came to seek our blessings.'

'All the same,' said Canny Kamran 'one does expect the Umranis to come more often to visit us.'

'People visit the dead,' Sufi Saeen said, 'when they wish to pray for their souls, or when they crave their help in achieving an elusive goal. Sometimes a sorrowful person pines for long at not being able to overcome a particular loss and assuages the grief by various gestures. Otherwise little else is exchanged between the living and the dead.

'That is the way it should be. God does not expect the living to live a life of mourning.'

'I expect you're right,' Artful Arbab said, 'but it makes one feel better to see the homage paid by Lady Ninette to Shahryar when she comes to Deriabad. She always leaves a rosebud along with her floral tribute.'

'As I mentioned,' Sufi Saeen remarked, 'that is an example of individual behaviour, not what is done as a matter of course.'

'I wish she'd leave an odd rosebud on my grave,' said Curiouso.

'She didn't know you, did she?' Sufi Saeen asked, 'then why should she bother?'

Sameera had also come to Deriabad ostensibly to cover the anniversary but in fact for two other reasons: to see Meheryar and to find out what she could about the missing patrol. While in the port city she managed to obtain a copy of the government gazette of 1876 which contained a report of the robbery in the palace committed by Hindu slaves.

Soon after her arrival, she called on the curator of the Deriabad museum seeking information about the robbery. The curator seated in a wheelchair, bent almost double with age, took ages to read the material she showed him. In a quavering voice he asked Sameera the reason for her inquiry. She told him of her interest in the missing patrol. The custodian whispered something to his two youthful assistants, and whipped the wheelchair around declaring that he would meet her at the same time the following day.

When they met again, he said, 'Some Hindus stole a crumpled up embroidered flag type fabric containing *ayas* from the Quran and a few utensils from an antechamber behind the throne room. The palace guards chased the thieves but they jumped off the balcony and rode away. They were followed for a few days until their trail was lost in the desert.'

Just then one of assistants approached with what looked like a tin box. The curator screwed his eyes and asked, 'What's this?'

'Sir, it has some items in it that you may wish to show the lady,' said the assistant.

The curator went purple in the face.

'Idiot, numbskull, fool,' he shrieked taking Sameera by surprise, 'I haven't said thing about this box. Don't touch it again without my instructions.'

Reverting back to her, he said, 'That's all there is about the robbery. It happened a long time ago. I have no more for you.'

'May I please study the source which records this event?' Sameera asked.

'Certainly not,' he snapped. 'No one can access the palace records without written authorization from the ruler.'

Later in that day Meheryar accompanied by Sameera paid a farewell call on Ninette and Rabby on the eve of their departure for the port city. In the salon, Sameera's attention was drawn to a book with a green leather cover embossed with gold lettering lying on a side tale. On enquiry, Ninette mentioned that it was one of a set of three volumes of special signifiance on the history of Deriabad and nine other interconnected states in the Subcontinent.

'Why is the book special?' asked Meheryar.

'Well for one it records that Deriabad existed in the tenth century. It is a collaborative effort of scholars from seven different historical sources: Subcontinental, Arabian, Persian, North African, Turkish, French and English. Despite language mismatches, they have drawn on indigenous original material, matched accounts where possible, highlighted unreconciled differences in preparing a fairly comprehensive account of history of the central Subcontinent.'

'Oh, this work was well known even before publication. Isn't Dr. Andre Moreau the coordinator?' asked Sameera.

'That's right. He started the project seven years ago ... in fact it was started by Al-Ghazali during the 11th century.'

'Good heavens, so long ago,' Rabby remarked.

'Ghazali died a few years later with the project unfinished.

His group of the scholars dispersed soon after since there was no one left to coordinate it and no funds forthcoming without him.'

'How did Dr. Moreau get into the picture?' asked Meheryar.

'He came upon the unfinished project amongst the archives at the Louvre.'

'There is a fascinating article on Dr. Moreau's revival of the project in The National Geographic and also an award winning documentary in the 'Discovery' series,' said Sameera.

'Andre's team has been at it for the last seven years, and finally some of the work is complete and ready for the world.'

'How did you get a copy Mummy?' Rabby asked.

'The publishers Guillamme and Guillamme, whom I know well, sent me a printers' copy of the first volume a few days ago.'

On turning the book's cover, Meheryar's noticed a phrase in nastalikh. He asked Ninette what it meant.

'I don't know the script well, but that is a slightly blurred facsimile of a hand written sentence in Persian ascribed to Al-Ghazali which says: "Look deep and you will see how people on the other side live"…'

The book was passed from hand to hand and looked at with great interest.

'Do you think it'll become a best seller?' Rabby asked.

'Probably not in the popular sense but certainly in academic and literacy circles,' said Sameera 'not only because of the subject, but the wealth of scholarly opinion.'

'I would go beyond that,' Ninette said, 'I believe that the significance lies in the contribution to the work by so many scholars since Ghazali's age. It is a living testament of a text that keeps on growing even a thousand years later.'

'Amazing,' said Meheryar, 'there are maps, letters, reproductions of busts and stone tablets.'

'There are also pictures of old structures, probably schools of law or parts of public buildings,' said Ninette.

'Oh, look,' said Sameera, 'there's a chapter on Deriabad.'

'Not just a chapter.' Ninette said, 'There's an entire section on it, from origin to post British times. It is so for many other states as well.'

'My interest,' said Sameera, 'would be in Deriabad during the 1870s onwards.'

'Why just the 1870s?' Ninette asked.

'Important things happened then. Actually they took place in 1876.'

'What things?' Rabby asked.

Sameera recounted the episode of the missing patrol.

'Are you poring over the Deriabad section of the book hoping some clue will pop up?' Rabby asked with a laugh.

'I wish it was as easy as that,' Meheryar replied. 'If only there were more visuals. The ones here are few and far in between.'

'We're lucky to have what we do. I think it's difficult to preserve original pictorial material over eleven centuries,' Ninette remarked.

After a while Meheryar said, 'Hey, this is odd. There is a tablet here with what looks like the *Durood Sharif* inscribed on it along with Swastikas in the four corners.'

'That's very odd,' said Sameera. 'The swastika is not an Islamic emblem, not known to be used anywhere on Islamic artifacts.'

Ninette was silent, thinking back. 'Well,' she said, 'I have an old scroll, which has both the Arabic script and swastikas along with Hindi style writing.'

'How interesting. What is it about?' Sameera asked.

'You can see it if you like. I brought it with me to show Badshah Begum.'

She asked Rabby to fetch the wooden chest given her in Paris, from the bedroom.

Because of its size, the paper scroll lying within was laid out on a billiard table. They gazed at it silently for a while.

Meheryar was the first to speak, 'I think it depicts the Satrangi Desert lying south westward to the palace. See here is the palace gate. The swastikas you mentioned Lady N, are they on this?'

'If you tilt your head and look at the scroll sideways you'll see them, all along the border and then down there on the domed thing,' Sameera said.

'Yes, I see them now. How did you get this Lady N?'

'It was left to me by your father.'

At his look of surprise she explained how she came by it.

'If it was among father's things, then it is of great importance – especially when coupled with Arnaud's remark that it held answers to some family riddles.'

'It is obvious that this scroll has been handled by Muslims and Hindus ... if someone could find me a magnifying glass, I could try to decipher the Devanagari text.' Sameera said.

'Surprise, surprise, do you know Devanagari?' Meheryar asked.

'To some extent.'

The hunt for the magnifying glass took time as it had to be fetched from the palace office.

Sameera pored over the text, paper and pen in hand making notations.

'This,' she said after a pause, 'is an account of certain events concerning a *chatri* (umbrella) which is a sacred artifact for the Hindus. The original version was told to a child, named Abhineshwar, who repeated it to his slave Imratu ... after that the writing is unclear or scuffed. It says that the event has been repeated a number of times, and this seems to be the twenty third version. There are some references to Hindu kings, constellations, episodes and territories which are not clear, but it appears that in the reign of a Kumbara ... et cetera, et cetera, et cetera ... at the time of a sun eclipse, foreign armies of an alien faith struck and ... can't make out what this is ... oh, yes ... when the holy Sadhu Saprudipaksha came out of the Amarpali temple to observe the battle, he saw a fluttering ball of green material rolling towards him. As he approached it, a gust of wind wafted it upward on to the swastika of the temple's dome, and there it stayed fluttering away. He fell to the ground and thanked Parmeshwar for sending his *chatri.*'

'Does *chatri* mean umbrella?' Ninette asked.

'The holy umbrella or the Lord's sunshade.'

'That's fascinating,' Ninette said. 'Is there more?' we can't have heard it all.'

'There is more but darn difficult to decipher.'

'Please try,' Rabby urged.

'There's a chunk here that I can't do anything with – it needs to be deciphered by an expert in Devanagari.'

'Read what comes after that – if you can,' said Rabby.

Sameera resumed, 'There were seven of them – fair hair, fair skin, and light coloured eyes. Their horses were fierce and blew fire from their nostrils. The largest among them leapt on the dome and climbed up. He kept screaming, "Musalman alam, Allah hu Akbar!" He snatched the green flier off the dome, breaking the swastika and made off with it. On the ground Saprudipaksha lay dead with his throat cut.'

They were all quiet after the rendering. Moments later, Sameera said, 'That was eerie. Any comments, Meheryar?'

'The thing that sticks in my mind is the reference to an alam, which also means a flying standard,' Meheryar remarked.

'Yes, me too, I was wondering about that,' Rabby said.

'Why, are you reminded of the standard that is all important to the family?' Ninette asked.

'Is there any more on the scroll that might be of help?' Meheryar enquired.

'There is other stuff here but it deals with crossing rivers and praying in the rain ... can't see anything else that concerns your interest. I've been over it twice,' Sameera said.

'What if ... what if ... it was the standard which was displayed on a banner of the Muslim force that got detached in the heat of the battle and was blown by the wind to the temple, where the sadhu took it as a sign from his god ... what if ... unable to bear the idea of their standard being on a temple, the Muslims went back later to take it by force?' Meheryar murmured.

There was a silence.

'Well, it doesn't sound too implausible,' said Ninette, 'considering the importance given by your father to the contents of the chest.'

'In which case I wonder where it got to?' Rabby asked.

'May be it was the standard brought to Deriabad by Umrani forefathers,' Meheryar said laughingly.

'You mean our standard which got stolen?' Rabby remarked.

'That was meant to be a joke,' Meheryar said.

Suddenly Rabby sat bolt upright gesticulating excitedly.

'Yes Rabby, what is it darling?' Ninette asked with concern.

'Supposing … just supposing that the standard which was stolen from the palace…' Rabby said, 'was the one taken from the temple.'

'You mean the one stolen from the palace by the thieves in Sufi Saeen's time?' Meheryar asked, incredulous.

'I mean if it was stolen by descendents of the same people from whom the Muslims took it. After all they also regarded it holy,' Rabby said.

'What you are suggesting,' Sameera said thinking aloud, 'is that the sadhu lost the standard when it was taken forcibly by the warring forces. After which it remained in Muslim hands until several hundred years later, when it was stolen from the palace by Hindu thieves.'

'Yes, that's about the gist of it,' said Rabby, relieved that her theory had been taken semi seriously.

'The ruler then sought the help of the British government to track down the stolen goods … and the patrol that went after it got lost in the desert …' Meheryar murmured, ruminating.

There was a long silence.

After a while Sameera said, 'There's something else, which may or may not have a bearing on all this.' She then described the somewhat excessive reaction of the custodian to the assistant's slip-up over the tin box.

More silence followed.

Finally, Ninette suggested that they should retire instead of fantasizing further and reassemble the next day before she and Rabby left for the airport for deciding whether anything more needed to be done.

The next day Meheryar said, 'I think all this information should be put before the ruler, Sartaj Bhaijan, and his views sought. After all this is a matter which concerns the state, and its gone beyond the level of individual interest.'

'What if he decides not to do anything about it?' Ninette asked.

'Well then, I think every individual is entitled to do what he or she thinks is appropriate.'

There was some more discussion about the matter, but since no one was clear as to the best move, and also what they would do if left to their own devices, they decided to inform Sartaj.

# Chapter 19

Lt. Gen. Altaf Sarfaraz sat up most of the night pondering over what steps to take to derail the government's Poverty Alleviation scheme. All routes considered by him ran aground on account of the strong official backing for the programme.

*'One way to defeat the scheme is to defeat the government, but this government is going nowhere in a hurry. The next best thing to do is to try and weaken the government so it starts faltering on its obligations – such as delays in repayment of instalments, lapses in fulfilling its obligations in time and blaming the other side for the lapse, falsifying some of the correspondence with foreign parties to create confusion, neutralising the projector directors to create a vacuum of executives.*

His planning was directed at fostering the kind of rightist mindset that would lead ultimately to the ushering in of an Islamic state. His links within and outside of government were with those who shared such views.

He came from a humble family of clerics living on farmland bordering two provinces. He lived, studied and absorbed an extremist form of tribal Islam. He wanted to become a cleric for teaching and propagating the religion, but the leader of his order wanted him to join the army and work his way to a position of authority from where he could inculcate extremist ideology into the run-of-the-mill version observed by the forces.

Altaf's progress took him along another route involving education, weaponry and intelligence. He found this more to his liking and stayed on to achieve the position he held. He was a stone's throw away from the Head of State, and his counsel was heard – and at times, followed by the governing body.

The call of the muezzin announcing the morning prayer disrupted his thoughts.

*Weakening the government is what must be done,'* he concluded rising for the morning prayers.

Back at his planning post, he realized that weakening the AVM was a non-starter at this stage of his mandate. The individuals in government actively pursing the programme were Princess Bisma, Ameer Bakhsh and Begum Zarina. Incapacitating any of them would seriously hobble the programme.

In view of the Deriabad connection of Bisma and Ameer Bakhsh, he called Malik Azad Khan to the capital for discussions. He tasked him with finding the vulnerabilities of both. 'I want to use the most effective means to intimidate or otherwise incapacitate them.'

Malik Azad, ever eager to help his patron suggested two or three stratagem concerning Ameer Bakhsh, but his suggestions vis a vis Bisma were not fool proof.

The general gave his approval to one of the measures proposed against Ameer Bakhsh, but warned Malik Azad to be very careful when executing it, and make sure that no one came to harm.

The gang that was selected to do the job was led by Malik Azad's jack-of-all-trades, the overseer. On the evening on which the move against Ameer Bakhsh was to be made, the overseer had a rendezvous with four of his henchmen at a sugarcane field near Pattanwala. After they were instructed, and had matched timings, they concealed themselves amid cane stalks at short distances from each other. The night was moonless and quite still except for the calls of cicadas. A hoophoe called – followed by silence, a fox's bark, some night bird's call – footsteps approached along a path between the cane fields. The footsteps neared the spot where the overseer was hidden. He stepped out and confronted the person who approached. It was Razia, Ameer Bakhsh's wife returning home with a pot full of curds.

'Where to in such hurry, Razia Bibi?'

'What is that to you?' she said, her heart catching in her throat. 'I'm on my way home. Now get out of the way and let me pass.'

'Not so fast Bibi,' said another emerging from a nearby spot.

'We have a message for your husband … tell him to stop participating in the 'Homes for the homeless' scheme otherwise he will be sorry for what we may do to his home, or to him or to you.'

'Get out of my way so I can go home and tell him,' Razia said angry and terrified at the same time.

'Sit and talk to us little bird for a while before going home,' said a third person reeking of alcohol.

'Dilawar,' the overseer cautioned him, 'we are not meant to do anything other than what I told you. Now let's go.'

'Not while I have the bird in my grip,' said Dilawar placing both hands on Razia's shoulders.

Razia flung the pot of curds on him and screaming loud for help she managed to pull out a little dagger from her girdle while he cursed her for dousing him with curds. Incensed, Dilawar went for her. She tried to make a run for it but was held back by the fifth man who was also inebriated.

Dilawar and the fifth man had her on the ground, tearing at her clothes, while she screamed, cursed and twisted her body. The overseer and others grappled with them trying to pull them off. Finally she struck out with the dagger with all her might at whatever came her way. There were shouts and yells, one claiming, 'The whore she got me.'

'Malik sahib did not want anything like this to happen.'

'She's torn open my face,' yelled the overseer.

'She's missed my balls but slashed my stomach,' grunted another.

Razia was overcome with fear and struggled fiercely for what seemed like ages. The continuous grappling her body was subjected to and the combined weight of the five men trying to hold her down prevailed finally. Her resistance gave up at last. The situation had become irreversible with her lying there motionless half naked and the men all around. Some sexually aroused, others determined to avenge themselves for the stabbing they had undergone.

Sometime later, when it was quiet again, Razia got up – eyes wide open, mouth shut tight – gathered her tattered clothes around her and set off like a robot in the opposite direction to her home. At first she walked slowly, then her steps became faster and faster and almost broke into a run. Her face was animated now, crying, screaming, panting, yelling. Each breath she took was like a stab. Hair wild and unleashed; her stomach churned and water dripped from her eyes, nose and mouth.

'Not me … not me … this is not Razia … this … this body is taken over by the devil … full of evil … full of the badness in the world … not the body of his wife … not that of their mother … Razia has been pushed out of her body … she is body less … will anyone recognise her … will You take her in dear God … You were there … You watched her body die … her soul drift … You gave her to the devil …

Then she saw what she was looking for. It was there among the cane fields. She cried 'Allah,' twice then crossed the shallow wall facing her and plunged straight in.

'You let her get raped!' Malik Azad yelled. 'You let this happen when I told you how far to go.'

The five stood facing him, eyes downcast palms together held up in supplication.

'She struggled and attacked us with a dagger. She cut my face from forehead to chin,' pointing to a bleeding swab on his face. 'She …'

'One woman could not be controlled by five men,' he got up and struck the overseer's bleeding face with a force that knocked him down. The man cried out in pain then began to sob uncontrollably.

'What became of her after you left her. Does anyone know where she has gone? Go back you swine, find her and bring her here. She must not get to her home. Go … now!'

Except for the overseer the other four rushed out.

'Stop your slobbering and tell me what happened.'

The overseer sat up, wiped his bleeding face then asked for water and recounted the event, answering all the questions raised by Malik Azad.

'You know what you have done? Given cause for a blood feud. If any of this gets out, I do not intend to be connected to it.'

'Forgive me Malik sahib, I am less than the dust under your feet … it was a mistake … everyone got carried away and I could not stop them.'

'Everyone you say … then tell me, who raped her?'

The overseer hummed and hawed, finally claiming to be not too clear because of the darkness and the dust kicked up by the struggle.

Malik Azad put a foot on his chest and knocked him down.

'You lying bastard' he said. 'You're telling me you don't know who was involved. Tell me now or I'll have acid poured on your wounds.'

'All four …all four of them *saeen.*'

'All four … and what about the fifth?'

'Tell me the truth,' he said striking his testicles with his knee.

The overseer doubled over with pain cried out, 'Me too *saeen.* I was also one of them.'

Hours later, when the four men returned they were quite shaken.

'Well,' said Malik Azad, 'where is she?'

'She … she …'

'Speak up, what about her?'

'She is dead,' Dilawar said.

'Dead!' said Malik Riaz not realising the implications.

'Yes Malik sahib, she jumped into a nearby well.'

'Are you sure?'

'Yes, we followed her trail to the well. Torn off shreds of her clothes were caught up on the stone wall girding the well. It was too dark to see the inside of the well. We called and dropped stones. We heard the stones hitting the water.

'Did anyone see any of this?'

'I don't think so Malik sahib.'

'Good, then I want all five of you to leave the area without delay and find temporary homes with your relatives not less than seventy five kilometers from here.

Razia's absence from the home did not cause concern. She did sometimes stay overnight at her aunt's place but she always sent word when doing so. This time however, there was no news of her stay over. Assuming it to be an oversight, Allah Bakhsh bolted the doors on the alien night and retired.

When there was no news till midday the next day, Masuda Mai sent an emissary to the aunt's. On learning that she was last seen the evening before on her way home, Masuda Mai raised an alarm. The entire countryside liked Allah Bakhsh and the Lasharis, so on hearing the call, groups of two or three persons set out to scour the land to locate Razia. Within the space of two hours, the events of the evening before were known to the police. It did not take along for land savvy peasants to retrace her journey. The smashed pot of curds, the uneven patches of land where the scuffling took place, bits and pieces of her ornaments that broke off and strips of her clothing, all had a tale to tell. Her haphazard footprints and shreds of clothing led the way to the well, and local divers brought up the final piece of evidence.

Initially, Allah Bakhsh had kept the news of her absence away from Ameer Bakhsh on the assumption that she would be back any moment. However, subsequent events made it essential to disclose everything. Ameer Bakhsh flew in that afternoon on being told that Razia was at death's door. When he got to Deriabad, his parents told him what had actually happened.

What followed were probably the worst moments in Ameer Bakhsh's life. Disgust, blinding rage, guilt, overwhelming grief and the notion that what was being told him was untrue surged through him. He wept for a while, comforted his children, shared the grief of his horror struck kin and went to the police station to identify Razia's remains. Having been in water, the body was swollen. He was also taken to the well where she took her life. The police had some questions, some of which he answered. All the while he kept wondering who had done this. Why was she made to suffer the bestiality. Why was he not there.

By the evening the news had spread countrywide. The wife of a prominent MPA had been raped and her body found in a well. Even in a country used to dramatic headlines, scandals and horror laden events, the news about Razia and Ameer Bakhsh came as a devastating blow.

Hearing the news on TV, brought tears to Bisma's eyes. The topic was on everyone's lips. It aroused a great wave of sympathy for Ameer Bakhsh and a resolution was passed in the House praying for the deliverance of Razia's soul, conveying the goodwill and sympathy of the MNAs to Ameer Bakhsh and condemning the perpetrators of the crime.

The burial was fixed for the following day. It seemed like most of Deriabad had turned up at Pattanwala to accompany the cortege. There were also several sympathisers from the capital:MNAs, colleagues from the PA programme, a personal representative of the AVM, and scores of Tehreek members.

Bisma and Begum Zarina did manage to find some time with Ameer Bakhsh. He met them, eyes downcast, withdrawn as if he was holding something back with great difficulty.

Since the AVM was taking an interest in the investigation of the crime, a high powered team had been appointed for the task. Peasants skilled in discerning soil patterns were assigned the task of locating material clues left by the attackers from the two sites in the sugarcane fields. They retrieved shards of the curd carrying pottery, broken bangles, buttons, an empty bottle of local whisky, cigarette butts, fragments of a torn letter addressed to Dilawar Bhai, a man's sandal, strips of material that seemed to have fallen off garments, fairly visible mobile cell phone numbers scribbled on the inner side of a cigarette packet

After questioning Ameer Bakhsh and his family members exhaustively, the investigators were of the opinion that the crime was either politically motivated or a chance crime of passion in which Razia had got enmeshed.

When the period of mourning was over, Ameer Bakhsh was back at his desk. Bisma noticed his presence when she walked in. She slipped him a note which said, 'Good to have you back.'

'I returned because of what I have learned here and of what I hope to learn.'

'Learned about what?' Bisma asked placing her hand inadvertently on his arm. At her touch his arm stiffened and she felt a charge run through her body, causing her to withdraw the hand with a suddenness making him sit up.

'About research, planning, organization, and execution ... but mostly about human relations.'

'That's interesting ... the last part ...'

'Life should be shared with those you love otherwise it withers. If I had known this before my last visit home, I would have shared my experiences with Razia so she could visualise my life here. I never shared anything with her. I never gave her anything. I always took and she gave. I never even got to know her well.'

'Stop this kind of talk. We can't undo what has happened.'

'Not much in it for her was there.'

'My maid says that after God, Razia worshipped you. She claimed that being your wife gave her all the happiness she could want.'

# Chapter 20

'It has been a while now since that atrocity was committed, and I do not have a final report on your findings,' the AVM thundered down the phone to the DIG. 'Yes, yes, I have seen the interim reports and the other notes exchanged, but so far nothing definitive ... ah, you have some leads. I want to hear about them.'

Initial enquiries revealed that thirteen persons had left the area that evening – which included Pattanwala, Mazarian Wali and all the settlements in between. Tracking each lead finally led them to a Dilawar Shigri whose name appeared on the scrap of a letter they had found at the site. Dilawar, who had decamped to Multan, was located, questioned then beaten black and blue, but divulged nothing on account of his fear of what Malik Azad would do to his family if he gave anything away.

They questioned all the thirteen without making a break-through. Then there was a stroke of luck. The cigarette packet discovered in the cornfield on which the cell phone numbers were scribbled had been purchased from a hole in the wall shop. The same telephone numbers appeared on the shop's signboard. The coincidence was noted by the investigator. On questioning the shopkeeper, he was informed that the cigarettes had been purchased by his old friend, the overseer.

The telephone numbers had been written by him on the packet at the bidding of the overseer, who promised to join him later for sharing a joint and downing some local liquor.

'That was the night of that attack on Mian Allah Bakhsh's daughter-in-law. God rest her soul in peace.'

'Did your friend return for the joint and the liquor?'

'No, he didn't. I was told that he had gone on an assignment for his boss.'

With proof in hand, it did not take much effort to break down the overseer. He was a coward, terrified by the prospect of imprisonment.

The crime was acknowledged, the perpetrators finally identified and taken in custody, but the motive was not clear. The finger now pointed at Malik Riaz, who waited in trepidation for the doorbell to ring. He had reported the developments to Lt. Gen. Altaf Sarfaraz who had greater grounds for concern.

When Malik Riaz was questioned by the DIG, he admitted his involvement, but made it clear that rape or molestation was not intended. When asked as to whether there were other planners of the deed. He said that he would give his answer only to the Chief of Army Staff.

His request was granted. At the conclusion of the enquiry Lt. Gen. Altaf Sarfaraz was held responsible for conspiracy.

The rapists were tried, convicted and hanged. Malik Riaz was imprisoned for seven years. Lt. Gen. Altaf Sarfaraz was relieved of his job and court martialled for conspiracy and master minding a plot against the interests of the state. At the intervention of the COAS, he was imprisoned for a token eight months as a longer term would have caused resentment amongst the tribes who belonged to the interprovincial region from which he hailed. The COAS managed to prevail upon the AVM to exempt him on the grounds of the often observed strategy that 'decisions of state are at times made subject to geo-political considerations.'

Anti-government elements entrenched in the state suffered a major setback on account of the fall of the Lt. General. An extended witch-hunt exposed many cells and operators. There were resignations, out of turn retirements, more trials and convictions. However, true to the intrinsic nature of mankind, undiscovered forces inimical to the governing order went into hibernation, waiting to strike like denizens of the deep at the sound of the clarion call.

On her next visit to Deriabad after the ruler's death anniversary, Ninette with Meheryar in tow, took the matter of the standard to Sartaj.

They had asked for Badshah Begum to be present, but there was no means of getting rid of the insufferable Kulsoom.

Starting from the delivery of the chest to Ninette in Paris, the events in entirety were relayed. When it was over, Badshah Begum sat back and said, 'What an adventure. It would make for a best seller.'

'Also, box office movie,' put in Kulsoom.

'Before we get carried way with the thrills and the adventure,' Sartaj said, 'perhaps we had better note down the events and characters, giving dates where possible and bring the matter up to the present before deciding whether anythings needs to be done.'

And so it transpired. A detailed account of the series of episodes trigged off by the tenth century event, was drawn up by Meheryar and Sameera.

One matter stuck out like a sore thumb – that was the curator's outburst upon the appearance of the tin box. The curator was summoned and questioned. He mumbled and fumbled and finally admitted that the box contained items left behind by the thieves which his predecessor had ordered him never to reveal in order to perpetuate the story that the standard had disappeared mysteriously. When opened, the box contained half a yard of torn off woven woollen fabric dyed green. Some portions of the fabric had embroidery in gold thread. The only readable portion said "Akbar". The fabric was in danger of coming apart even with gentle handling. There was also a kirpan with a curved blade, a chopped topknot of grizzled white and grey hair, some beads and a piece of wood with Devanagari script appearing on it which said: "Bhagwan gives and takes. What you took from us, he has given back". Under that an attempt to blacken some earlier writing on the wooden slat did not entirely conceal the words "Amarpali Temple".

The curator was reprimanded and dismissed without pension by Sartaj for distorting history and conspiring to present historical events other than as transpired. Sartaj called it academic dishonesty of the worst kind.

Sartaj ordered a contingent of seven guards led by a captain to proceed to Amarpali temple in Satrangi Desert to search for and recover whatever remained of the standard and other palace artifacts found there.

'I can't see the central government taking any interest in the recovery of the standard since that is an individual state's private concern,' Sartaj remarked. 'I could make out a case for government involvement on the charge of theft of a religious antiquity, but it would complicate matters to involve it at this stage. I think we can handle it better on our own.'

'Your Highness,' Mehboob Alam Shah said, 'there are members of the royal family and others who want to join the expedition.'

'Yes, I am aware of that and I'm inclined to let them go. After all it is a family matter, and an unusual family matter for which I think there are no guidelines of conduct. They do realize that travel will be by SUV as there are no roads ... and the terrain is rough. As far as I know, Prince Meheryar has volunteered to go. There are some ladies too, I believe.'

'Well Highness, we have the lady journalist Sameera Rehman and Princess Rabia Sultan.'

Ignoring Kulsoom's whispered instructions, he said, 'Yes, they may all go. I'm sending two more guards who are proficient in the Satrangi dialect and will take special care of the princess.'

'Hurray,' said Rabby, 'for Bhaijan for letting us go.'

'Probably wants to be rid of you,' Ninette said laughing.

Later Badshah Begum said to Sartaj, 'That was noble of you.'

'Amma Huzoor, the standard was lost during the reign of an Umrani ruler, who people look up to as a saint. Well, we have some idea of the truth now. So let it be recovered in the reign of another, however insignificant he may be. At least he will be remembered by posterity,' Sartaj said with a half smile.

'If the standard is there and if whoever has it knows that we want it,' he mentioned to Meheryar, 'they may not give it up without a struggle or a battle. I don't want any unpleasantness to take place. So I am sending a box of silver coins with you to use if necessary.'

'What if it is in tatters or non-existent?'

'I want you to bring back whatever you find. If it is non-existent, at least we will be remembered for having resolved the mystery of the missing standard.'

'Are you sure you're going to be all right?' Ninette asked Rabby.

'Ever since that lunch at Mama Satrangi's I have been looking forward to the day when I could feel part of the land. It's all happening except I can't see us retrieving the standard which is probably a bundle of rags now … I shall be more than all right Mummy. My brother is leading the expedition and then there is Sameera whose experiences as a newsperson have made her one woman commando. The guards, I believe have been hand picked by Sartaj Bhaijan himself. They have a good idea about the lay of the desert … but there is something more.'

'Something more, what's that?'

'It would have been marvellous if Sadie had been here to go with us. I do miss her.'

'I miss her too,' said Ninette, 'but she's doing her own thing, travelling around the world with Hussain.'

'If not Sadie, then I wish a friend of mine called Kamal Alam could share this experience'.

'Oh, you mean the archaeologist you introduced me to at the port city?' Ninette remarked

'Yes, his archaeological soul would be thrilled'

'That's a tall order,' Ninette said, 'but let's see what can be done … well, I suppose you'll be in good hands.'

Sameera cautioned her newspaper and Tasveer-e-Watan to maintain confidentiality about the expedition. 'One word to the media, and everyone will come chasing across, with helicopters to make the first scoop.'

'Smart girl,' said Meheryar making a mental note of her instinct to anticipate good coverage in the offing.

'I want Xerxes and an assistant flown down to Deriabad laden with plenty of portable digital photographing and audio/video recording equipment for spectacular footage, if I'm right, that will have National Geographic, Animal Planet and all major nature coverage outlets rooting for more,' she instructed her sources hastily at their port city bases.

# Chapter 21

There was a buoyancy in the corridors of government. Its performance had been moderately successful of late which is a rarity at the best of times as bureaucratic passages customarily echo to the stomping of club feet.

Unknown to many, the AVM's chosen fields of study were governance, movement of capital and differentials in the prices of the major resources. He had kept abreast of the latest developments in these fields since his postgraduate research days.

He had been navigating the ship of state skillfully, skirting the pitfalls and benefiting from the upturns. His years of study had alerted him to the knack of predicting trends in world affairs. This was of great help when he planned government strategy. He was not oriented towards consumerism, nor did he support the commodotizing trend. He had strong reservations about capitalization as well as the scramble for market control but he knew that the game had to be played according to the ground rules of the capitalist order otherwise his country would have to face sanctions that only China and Russia could withstand but would turn any other country into an international pariah.

'Its not a fair world,' he said to Bisma, 'but it's the only one we have and we have to live it out.'

'God's plan foresaw a fair world,' she retorted.

'Did it?' the AVM countered. 'He put those characters Cain and Abel in it, and look what they did. Fairness went up into space there and then. Anyway we have to play with blemished hands and tricks up our sleeves, to keep ahead of the sharks. We can seek God's dispensation afterwards.'

'Your point's taken sir,' the Finance Minister said impatiently. 'We'll play by your ground rules.'

'While I'm about it, there is something for the F.O. too: our foreign friends who remain as our friends will continue to enjoy the attention we have always given, but there has to be a change in strategy. We will cosset our friends to the extent that they keep faith with us. Any wavering, or preference for another country, must be dealt with in the same way. I do not think it is good policy to treat some countries as more special than others. This attitude is partly sustained by the press. We must give the press strict guidelines about our approach. No more over the top statements about death and sacrifice to the last man. Your country comes first, more so than any other. This is the only country that God gave us.'

Critics commented on the AVM's bravado and wondered when he would fall foul of the rightists. But he was no novice, this man. He kept the traditionalists and their funds on a tight leash, releasing them only when they cooperated with him.

Opposing political interests had tried to forge some form of unity to face him, but the game was lost before it began. He was popular with the masses. They were at one with him in the belief that the best form of government was democracy monitored by a controlling dispensation. It seemed to be working.

News travelled. It did not take long for the plus points of the new regime to be noticed. The economic outlook was brighter, the currency firm, the balance of trade favourable, employment was on the upturn, crime had fallen by twenty seven percent, frauds, hoaxes and scams had all but disappeared. Corruption and nepotism were the hardest nuts to crack. Perseverance was the order of the day.

Perhaps the most important indicator was public opinion. And that showed signs of optimism, a revival of faith in the governance of the country and a looking forward to better days.

Commentators and opinion makers had found a new subject to extol: a revival of sound governance in the Subcontinent that could lead to a resurgence of the region. Some had gone further making much of stature of the AVM on account of his academic predisposition, middle of the line proactivity and technocratic acumen, which they felt marked him out from middle ranking South Asian leaders for a place amongst the exemplary statesmen of the decade.

He was now in a transitory phase of his vision. He wanted his ministers and the media to inspire the working classes to exercise their mental capacities. The struggle for work and food were a primary concern, but the mental capacity of the average citizen of the lower middle and poor classes was a dead asset.

'There has to be a way to egg these unthinking millions to become creative mind users,' he said at a committee meeting. 'Our regular affairs of state are in hand, and we are here to deal with any unexpected turn, but my concern today is to push our citizenry to a higher level of existence.'

'For that there is education,' the Minister for Education said.

'Yes there is, but despite the huge outlay we've made to your ministry, our spread of education is too meagre and it does not go to the level where it becomes a practical asset.'

'What are you proposing sir?' Ameer Bakhsh asked.

'At the moment I am talking at random, and those of you who are in my think tank I hope to take along with me.'

'Your random observations have included many subjects. Do we have an agenda for any of them?' Begum Zarina asked.

'No, no agenda, just a committee *gup shup* – chat session – between old friends about some of the things we need to do.'

The reference to *gup shup* raised a few eyebrows and brought a smile to Ameer Bakhsh's face.

'I've been keeping a memo on the policy initiatives you have raised from time to time,' Begum Zarina said. 'Would it help now if I referred to it, and we take up items for discussion from it.'

'Begum Sahib, that's a good idea. Whatever we speak of should be recorded as a basis for further discussion in cabinet.'

'One of your earliest suggestions was related to a foreign policy approach. That we treat our allies with the same consideration they give us. No more special relationship or gratuitous courtesies.'

'Yes, I remember that. Didn't go down well in the F.O. they have their favoured foreigners.'

'It went down very badly with you know who.'

'We almost became persona non grata,' the Foreign Minister said.

'But you see how quickly it has settled down,' the AVM said. 'It was more a snarl than a roar and it had the desired effect. Not finished yet though. I shall be sending more memos on that matter to the F.O.'

'Anyway there's much less pussyfooting and playing courtier to visiting dignitaries,' said the Finance Minister.

'Then,' Begum Zarina said, 'we've been encouraged to prompt the working classes to exercise their mental capabilities and rise to a higher level of existence.'

'These are issues I would like all of you to raise whenever the opportunity arises, especially in public meetings or in statements to the press. Talking often helps promote views as effectively as any documentary.'

'Sir, some of these things are difficult to communicate. There are no books or training courses to follow on elevating levels of existence.'

'You can make them aware of the advantage of using the mind either by explanation or giving actual examples. Try to explain it in relation to practical matters like cooking food, looking after a sick person, feeding a child, turning off the electricity or a tap of running water. Take it up in matters of dress, cleanliness and appearance.'

'Sir,'said the Accountant General, 'we have so much clutter and wrongdoing to sort out before we can undertake welfare projects.'

'Look, we have to start with fundamental matters first. There is no leap forward into a modern future without going through preliminary steps. After the industrial revolution, most result oriented equipment except for that which could be updated from earlier models to cope with progress had to be innovated in or transported into Western countries. It will have to be introduced here the same way. At the time of installation, systems or methodology to run the equipment were also introduced by the innovators. This combination resulted in the success of mechanization.'

'That is how the advanced countries progressed,' said the Minister of Finance and that is what we must do if we wish to modernize. We can borrow from them, learn from them, copy them, but in the end it has to be our effort.'

'Instant modernism has happened in the Gulf (mechanically at least if not temperamentally) but is unlikely to occur again,' said the AVM. 'I don't know how real the Gulf experience was for the locals but when we were building our country before and after the British occupation, we lived through the experience. Now we seem to have turned away from that approach. We seem to be unlearning everything we learned. The plants are rundown, the machinery is idle, the spare parts are the wrong specification. No one runs his affairs systematically. So I fear we are going backward to a time when the country will be run by a handful of superhumans who will rule over a computerized populace that will do as it is asked, think as it is instructed and live as it is ordered.'

The discussion continued in this vein until it was time to adjourn for prayers. Two matters of practical purpose were decided. The success of the home for the homeless programme required greater publicity. Begum Zarina was appointed to lead a delegation to the eastern and southern regions of the country and address public meetings. Bisma was also appointed to lead a delegation to the north and western regions for the same purpose.

The venue for Bisma's public meeting was in the neighbourhood of the railway station of the largest north–western city. It was a vast swathe of land for which the city fathers had hatched and dumped many plans. Parts of it were – as in cases of other such plots – under illegal occupation Wooden posts linked by rope or barbed wire cordoned off plots claimed by illegal occupants. The site was ablaze with lights focusing on a stage with three sides open to enable large numbers of spectators to participate. Gigantic projector screens had been erected at a great height around the stage. At the centre of the stage there was the speaker's podium with the audio equipment. Three steps below the podium a lower sage had been set up for the performers. Everything was in place for the show.

It began with the skits and song and dance numbers performed by reasonably well known artistes. It was mostly pop stuff to which the crowd responded. The first batch of speakers were also known to the crowd who cheered and clapped. While they spoke a black limousine wove its way through the mass and made its way towards the stage. Bisma dressed in customary white with a *chaddar* stepped out followed by a lady MNA. A cry of 'Baji' —sister— which was the name the masses had coined for her, went up. 'Baji has come,'was repeated by the crowd.

Ameer Bakhsh dismounted from the front of the car. She made her way swiftly up the steps to the stage accompanied by the music of 'Sohni Dharti' with the crowd singing along. On the podium the earlier speakers stood up and hailed her. The crowds cheered wildly and she waved back. It lasted for minutes on end. She had to raise her arms for a final wave before sitting down.

The main speeches were to be given by Bisma, Ameer Bakhsh and another MNA. Ameer Bakhsh came to the microphone, recited a few lines from the Quran in which man is advised to make use of the good things given by nature. He went on to disclose some technical aspects of the project, starting with the problems the builders faced from preparation of the land to the completion of a house. He also dwelt on the ancillary benefits of such projects: road networks, commercial activities, shops and markets, schools and dispensaries, electricity and water supply, parks and playgrounds, control centres run in conjunction with the local authority to monitor the functioning of all areas of the project, emergence of civic pride and communal leadership. As he spoke, images of such facilities flashed on the screens. The speech by the other MNA was brief as it had to be, given the number of voices calling out for 'Baji.'

Ameer Bakhsh raised his eyes to take in the tall, slender figure when she stood up, and then lowered them as she said, 'My fellow citizens, Assalam alaikum' – the voice was louder, clearer, authoritative, still resonant, well modulated, convincing.

'Wa-alaikum assalam, Baji,' they yelled back.

'You have already heard my colleagues speak on the different aspects of the housing scheme so I am not going to talk to you about its benefits and what it can do for you. Instead I am going to discuss the need for many extensions of the project. For each person who has been housed, there are a thousand more who need to be housed. How would we answer the Maker if we were asked: you supplied housing for a million persons, how about the hundred million more who are still homeless?'

An aerial shot of the pilot project flashed on the screens raising a chorus of 'oohs' and 'ahs.' A long shot showed houses extended to the far extreme of the screen with a tiled portion of each roof shaded either red, or green or blue to dispel the visual monotony of identical houses standing side by side on long stretches of land. A panoramic shot of the site showing children playing in open areas, people walking about and transport plying the roads, made it look like a toy shop display of a housing colony.

'This is just one of them,' she said. 'There are three others under construction, and we plan to have many more in the coming years. So I have come here to ask you for something.'

They waited. After a pause she said, 'Give me this land on which we stand tonight. We will build such a project on it, and it will become a source of pride for you for giving something so valuable to your fellow citizens. The example we have set in this country is being followed by other countries who have similar housing problems. Doesn't it make you proud to be a leader by example.'

'Baji,' called out a voice, 'are you doing anything like this in Deriabad?'

'I have donated two one hundred acre parcels of land, and members of my family have also done so. Our entire contribution exceeds several thousand acres...'

A shot rang out. Bisma slumped forward hanging on to the microphone for a minute. There was silence, broken by pandemonium. Ameer Bakhsh sprang up, pushing people aside frantically to get to her. Kneeling beside her, he held up her head with one hand, placing the other under her shoulder blades. She had been shot on the left side of her chest. Blood spurted forth mingling with Ameer Bakhsh's tears. A doctor on the scene rushed to the microphone telling those on stage to stay put until she was carried away. Unnecessary movement he yelled, would be harmful for her. Time was of the essence.

Soon there was uncontrolled commotion at the site. People wailing, women screaming, a babel of voices calling out, police sirens whining. Crowds pushing to get out, some trying to get on to the stage, volatile pressmen everywhere, people resorting to fisticuffs and a general free for all.

Without waiting for the medicos to arrive, Ameer Bakhsh lifting her up as gently as he could manage, went down the stairs with her, while onlookers stood aside. At that point Bisma opened her eyes and made as if to sit up.

'Bibi, please you've been shot,' Ameer Bakhsh said.

'I'm alright, Ameer Bakhsh,' Bisma said, 'it's a surface wound.'

While they talked he kept moving towards the car which was ready to go. He saw, standing beside the car, amid the onlookers, a man raise what looked like a nozzle aimed at Bisma. He whipped around, thrust Bisma into the arms of the surprised doctor and leapt on the man. The man panicked and tried to break loose, but was prevented from using his right hand which held the gun under a cloth. Ameer Bakhsh snatched it away from him and punched him savagely.

By now the police were in the picture. They led the man away. They also waved batons rounding up several others. The car jerked forward. Led by a police escort it careened to one of the advanced city hospitals. Emergency arrangements were activated. Messages had gone out to reputed specialists located within reach to get to the hospital without delay.

Bisma was still conscious when they got to hospital. She was rushed into the operating theatre where her wound was exposed. It was too close to the heart. After an hour's delay the young surgeon in charge decided not to wait for a specialist but to proceed without delay.

He burrowed away and got to the bullet. At this point, one of the specialists arrived, but he did not want to interrupt the surgeon who had by now extracted the bullet and patched up the wound. The specialist complimented him on what he called 'a first rate job.' Later on, to media representatives, he said, 'This young man has saved the life of one of our future leaders.'

Outside the operating theatre, Ameer Bakhsh kept vigil pacing the corridor restlessly. When at last endurance threatened to give way, he murmured into cupped hands, *No harm shall come to you as long as I live. I vow that from this day forward, I will be by your side. I seek nothing from you other than being allowed to protect you. In doing so, I shall not transgress on your life or dignity in any manner whatsoever.*

# Chapter 22

The Amarpali Temple was estimated as being at a distance of eighty five kilometers from Deriabad. Assuming that the average speed of the vehicle on that terrain would be approx fifteen kilometers per day, the round trip was estimated to last ten days but there was leeway for more time. Two SUVs carrying Meheryar's group and the guards were to be followed by a van stocked with extra tyres, essential spare parts, weaponry, food, first aid provisions, bedding rolls and personal belongings and a hitched on power generator. Water and fuel carrying bowzers brought up the tail of the caravan.

The expedition had been held up on account of the assassination attempt on Bisma. It had taken a week for the country to settle down to some sort of norm after the incident. Promise of early recovery had raised the hopes of her well-wishers. Much to the surprise of Rabby, Kamal Alam turned up a day before the expedition set off.

The departure took place after morning prayers. It was a good time to start before the sun came up. The lead driver veered off from the outer road girding Falaktaj palace on to the uneven ruggedness of Satrangi. From that point onwards it was a bump and grind run, stopping frequently to avoid a ditch or a landfall. There was no road except for the hint of a track which was used by horses, mules and men. So in a sense a motorable route, aided by the map on the scroll was being charted for the first time.

The vehicles stirred up a great deal of dust which the air-conditioning of the SUVs was not fully equipped to deal with. As the sun came up lighting up the further regions of the desert, it revealed an ochre coloured landscape with rocky accumulations, gnarled and twisted tree stumps pointing upward like dead fingers, desert thistle and other thorny bushes. The land was not even. As far as the eye could see it was pitted with dips and hollows and mounds of coppery hillocks. Other than occasional birds in the sky and scurrying creatures in the undergrowth there was nothing living in sight. They were navigating with the help of a compass and a global positioning system. Guards who had some familiarity with the desert were an added help.

Things went fairly evenly till lunch time. They stopped close to a hilly range marked on the map. A water source shown on the site turned out to be a gusher of bubbling muddy water which had been used as a rubbish dump.

For lunch they preferred sandwiches and ready-made food instead of a meal cooked by the guards. Rabby went off to relieve herself in seclusion, as did Sameera. Within a few minutes horrific screams were heard from Rabby's site. While the men dithered, Kamal picked up a stick and reached her in a flash. She was standing mesmerized above two snakes entwined in copulation. Kamal pushed her away and waved the stick at the snakes. One disappeared in the undergrowth, whilst the other took an aggressive stand. Kamal kicked some sand on it and backed away sufficiently for it to move away.

Rabby was so shaken by the experience that Kamal had to hold her until she calmed down.

They drove on through the afternoon chatting, occasionally breaking into song and dozing in turn. Meheryar and Sameera talked of childhood memories – he recounted instances of what if was like being brought up in Falaktaj palace. They laughed a great deal, and traded jokes. He even succeeded in getting her to join in a namaz by way of a dare.

Rabby spoke about the casino and the accident in Paris. She mentioned how traumatised they were – 'like being criminals, without having committed a crime.' She mentioned some of the games they played with the paparazzi. On one occasion, Sadie and she, took advantage of their identical appearances, to dress alike on a visit to a well known store. The paparazzi followed her until she disappeared in a changing room. At a prearranged signal Sadie, appeared at the opposite end of the store causing confusion amongst the reporters.

Come evening and they would get busy with their cell phones to loved ones until the signals ceased. The evenings in the desert were the best part of the day. The heat of the day gave way to a breezy coolness. The sunsets were spectacular, lighting up the western sky in all shades of red, orange, yellow. The sound of cicadas or night birds or an occasional call by a fox, broke the silence. The guards would light a fire and cook a tasty meal under stars emerging one by one. When the sun was truly gone, the sky was a canopy unlike any other. It was studded with the largest, the brightest and the greatest number of stars ever assembled. The travellers lay on bedding rolls outside tents on a hill, chatting and looking up at the sky until the day's tiredness got to them and they drifted off to sleep. The silence of the night was haunting.

After two days there was a change in the weather. Gusts of wind whipped up fine sand and assailed the travellers like stinging mites. It was no longer possible to sleep in the open. The guards put up tents for them. They were awakened one day by a sandstorm. The sand hit exposed parts of the body like a whiplash. Visibility was almost zero. Powerful gusts buried all exposed objects in cascades of sand. All they could do was to huddle together in a tent and push out sand accumulating at base of the tent.

The following day was warm but temperate. The SUVs, van and bowzers had to be dug out from the mounds surrounding them. Their immediate landscape had changed. There were sand drifts and landslides where there had been none and hillocks where there had been flat land. Not much progress was made with the journey as the vehicles had been affected by flying sand. There were enough hands to deal with the vehicles and the presence of two car mechanics was helpful.

Xerxes kept busy taking pictures of the unusual terrain, of the men digging up the vehicles, or of anything he found interesting. Meheryar who had never encountered so much sand before, decided to rag Rani Satrangi.

'Mama,' he said on the radio phone, 'you have a formidable presence here. You're all over us, drowning our bodies, choking our throats, riding with us in the vehicles during the day and an unwelcome companion in our tents at night.'

She laughed, 'So now you know not to take us too lightly ... we were the original rulers from whom your ancestors snatched Satrang territory ... tell me son how is the water holding out?'

He reassured her about the water situation. 'We even have enough for baths.'

'How far have you reached?'

'We are almost at half way point.'

'By the way, how long will we be able to continue talking this way?'

'Don't worry Mama, we have a charger with us, and if we lose signal contact we can communicate directely by radio,'

'Must say, Sartaj has equipped you well.'

'Yea, it must be Badshah Begum's influence.'

'Whatever it is, bless him for his goodwill.'


During the stopover, Sameera wandered off for a walk.

'Look what I've found,' she called.

Meheryar went over to look at a light chocolate coloured vixen half covering a hole lined with thistle leaves containing four tiny, tiny bundles of fluff yelping and squealing. Sensing that Sameera did not want to harm her pups, the vixen continued licking them.

After a while they wandered off in the direction of a lone tree sprouting unusual looking flowers.

'We've never been together for a walk before,' Meheryar said.

'It feels kind of nice,' she said.

'What the walk or being with me?'

'You know the answer to that.'

'How come you never ask questions of what work I do?'

'Why would I do that?'

'Because you are interested in me, and should want to know all about me,' he said with laughter.

'What conceit you have ... are all princes so conceited?'

'No, this one is single-minded. He knows who likes him and whom he likes. He also knows that the liking started sometime ago on a boat!'

'You sensed something then?'

'Yes.'

'How could you possibly have known my reactions at the time?'

'By the way you sought me out, looked at me, spoke to me, the subjects you chose to discuss. That wasn't chat, it was banter ... what Shakespearian lovers do.'

'And you, how was it with you?'

'How could it have been? I was with you all the time, looking at you, responding to you, waiting for your return to Deriabad. Playing truant with my work responsibilities to catch a glimpse of you.'

'Why didn't you say anything?'

'There are right times to say things. Like now, when we are away from the palace and others. With nothing but the desert and natural elements.'

He took her in his arms and kissed her.

'Is there anything more you want to know?' he asked.

'No, she said,' shaking her head, 'its all just been said.'

After a while he said,

'Listen I am not just an idle prince living on family largesse. Any idea what I do?'

'I know already. You are the CEO of the Umrani agricultural enterprises, both farms and industries. You cultivate crops and export and market cereal, grain, sugar and bulk cotton and ... fruit and vegetables and are also a leading member of an international body that oversees, fruit and vegetable festivals.'

Meheryar's eyebrows remained up in surprise, 'How come you know all this?'

'I am not a newspaper researchist without purpose,' Sameera said, 'besides, I had to be sure as to what was in store for me in case I said yes.'

The vehicles were functional by the early afternoon. Meheryar suggested they should leave soon as possible to get close to a grove of trees shown on the map which would give them access to the temple. While the van was being manoeuvered into a drivable position, an awkward reversal found it teetering on the brink of an unexpected landfall. Off loading the extra trappings and combining the strength of the men and women, with the tugging of the SUV's pulling in the opposite direction along with reverse acceleration by the van, drew it back from the pit.

Unable to travel that day, they set out early the following morning. On the way they encountered some goats and what looked like oversize iguanas. The guards sensed the presence of men and kept a wary eye. Rabby had developed a slight temperature. A concerned Kamal hovered around attending to her needs. He placed her head on his lap and kept the sand flies, mites and the burning rays of the sun away from her face.

That afternoon they checked out their direction with the help of the compass and the global positioning system and pointed their convoy in the direction of Amarpali. They had no idea as to what lay ahead nor any coordinated plan of action when faced with what lay ahead.

Rabby was the first to notice a change in the dynamics. On the right side of their SUV, three Satrangi warrior like figures on horse back stood in a row. They were bare bodied except for loincloths. Their hair was matted and long. It was covered with a headgear of fur, feathers, beads and boar's tusks. They held a spear in one hand and a shotgun in the other.

One of the two guards familiar with their dialect took Meheryar's permission to speak to them. He greeted them and offered good wishes.

The central warrior figure responded in rasping tones: 'Who are you? What are you doing here where strangers do not come? Where have you come from? What do you want?'

'We have come from Deriabad across the desert,' the guard said, as instructed by Meheryar. 'We came here looking for you and have the honour of standing on your ground. We are looking for a way to put an end to any animosity between us.'

'You are brave to have travelled across the desert. We do not welcome strangers. What is the animosity you refer to?'

The travellers conferred amongst themselves. Finally, the guard repeated Meheryar's words: 'We are tired and thirsty. We need to rest before further talk.'

The three warriors conferred, and then one in a high pitched nasal voice said, 'We will take you to our chiefs who will decide what is to be done.'

After a half hour of following the horses the travellers saw before them an octagonal structure with a melon shaped dome.

Fluttering from the pinnacle was what looked like shredded green remnants of the standard rended threadbare by centuries of exposure to the weather.

This was the Satrangi stronghold. The natives were olive skinned, tall and lean. Some walked about near the base of the temple. Some went in and out of quarters built along the periphery of the temple. They were curious but not nosy about the strangers. The travellers got out of the vehicle and walked slowly towards the temple. Some guards stayed behind in the vehicles.

On the blowing of a conch shell, a very old man with a beard inches above the floor came out of the temple and walked with a crutch instinctively towards Meheryar. He held out his hand and Meheryar took it in both his hands. 'I think it's the high priest,' he mumbled.

'This,' said the guard, 'is the Nawab Shahryar's, son Meheryar.'

There was an audible sound of 'ahhh.' 'He is also the son of Rani Satrangi.' That was enough to get a dozen or more conch shell sounds blowing through the still air, causing natives to emerge from barely visible terracotta quarters on terraces in hills surrounding the temple and gravitate towards the temple.

'Is it war?' asked one. 'Don't know, some important person has come to the temple.' 'Perhaps the priest has died.'

The speculation stopped when they saw Meheryar standing within the precincts of the temple, magnificent, bare chested, draped in a cloak of shells, feathers and beads, with high rising headgear and plumes which trailed like the wings of a bird, a golden spear in his hand and beads and shells of different shapes and hues arrayed on his torso. A Satrangi of the ruling order had come home. Meheryar felt humble and honoured. The head priest explained the significance of Meheryar's visit to his people. Men, women, children came in droves to touch his knees as he stood in the courtyard.

Xerxes kept busy capturing all that they saw in digital snapshots and videos, while Sameera jotted in note books whenever she could.

The celebration of Meheryar's 'homecoming' lasted till evening. There was communal dancing and singing. Not for a moment did the priest overlook his responsibilities as a host. The visitors were served a nutty milk cocoction, fruit juice, even locally brewed beer and date wine. They were offered barbecued sand grouse, quail and roasted rabbit followed by fruit and vegetables, cooked or sun-dried. A lotus like plant became popular as did birds wings dipped in honey. The visitors were even provided washing and sleeping facilities.

After that it was time to talk. Meheryar, via his interpreter, gave a comprehensive account of the saga starting with the arrival of the Muslim forces and ending with the theft in 1876 of the standard.

Then the priest narrated his version of events. The Satrang Desert had always belonged to the tribe. In the tenth century –indicated by ten fingers – raiders from the West conquered most of the land and brought with them a new religion. They were not prepared to live in peace and chose to destroy what they found alien. The priest handed two clay tablets, to Meheryar. One depicted a horse being ridden by a chalk faced foreigner flaunting a fluttering cloak. The second one showed a foreigner ordering a Satrangi to let go the reins of the horse. The foreigners had large eyes and flowing hair. The priest explained, 'These tablets contain our history.'

On the night before the invasion by the Allah worshippers, the keeper of the Amarpali Temple, High Priest Saprudipaksha dreamt that hostile forces were coming but that the Lord would send his umbrella to Saprudipaksha as a sign that the all would be well. And that came to pass. As the invaders struck, a measure of thick green fabric was blown by the wind towards him. On reaching him, the *chatri* opened its wings like a bird and was wafted to the top of the dome. Saprudipaksha dropped on his fours thanking his god for the sign. Two days later the fabric was dragged down and taken away by the invaders. A clay tablet depicted a foreigner tugging at the standard while Saprudipaksha lies prostrate on the ground.

The Satrangi tribal chiefs then took a decision to secure their people by withdrawing into the desert. The central area of the desert falling on the other side of the hills was habitable and had good water sources. They retreated to the central bowl, leaving the outer fringes of the desert as hostile terrain to secure themselves from intruders.

Several tablets depicted the abundance of crops in the new habitat. One depicted a high priest paying respects with a tribute of gifts to what seemed like a nawab like figure on a throne. The priest explained that on the inception of Umrani role in Deriabad, some priests called on the ruler as a matter of courtesy.

Centuries later, four Satrangi youngsters set off on an escapade and found themselves in Deriabad. They were captured by guards and put to work in a palace as slaves. An accidental handling of some green fabric displayed behind the throne by one of the boys earned him a severe beating from the guards.

'We tore it off your temple top and brought it here,' he was told by one of the guards. 'Praises of Allah, are written on it. Your touch will soil it.'

On a dark night, the four stole horses from the stables, dismantled the fabric and made off. On their return, the retrieved fabric was draped once again on the temple dome with great ceremony. The priest displayed a tablet showing the four, with a rolled up bundle.

There was no further dealings with Deriabad until years later, when Nawab Shahryar saw Rani Satrangi on an air flight to the port city and despite her having received offers for marriage from Hindu princes in the Subcontinent, he convinced the government and her father that they were meant for each other. A tablet commemorated their union.

There was a long silence after that.

'I think it is late, Prince,' the priest said finally,

'We should rest now and discuss this in the morning.'

And that was how they left it.

'There is no point resorting to hostilities,' Meheryar said at their morning meeting. 'Disputes should be settled by discussion. Too much time has passed, too many centuries gone by to justify revival of animosity, to cause bloodshed over symbols that don't touch the lives we lead today.'

'You speak like a Satrangi Prince … but then that is what you are. For the Satrangi, removal of the *chatri* would be like losing a member of the family. It would indicate that force can prevail over justice. It would signify that there is a faith held superior to ours.'

The priest then asked, 'How many people in the palace are grieved by the absence of the *chatri*? How live an issue is it there? With us it is an every day reality.'

'We know that there are holy words on the fabric. That makes it special. But it is revered by us also. It is a praiseworthy offering to the One that all subscribe to, Hindu and Allah worshippers. We do not feel that because it bears words from their book, it should be dishonoured. We believe that it is the Lord's *chatri* and so it must be revered. As long as it covers the dome, Satrang will survive. You take the *chatri* away from the dome, you take away Amarpali's specialness, you take away the heart of our settlement … you take away a home for the Satrangis … you destroy us.'

'The standard stays,' Meheryar said, 'and anyone who wants to pay respects may travel here for that. I myself will come here every year to see all is well. After all, I belong here as much as I do there.'

Meheryar's words made the Head Priest weep. Meheryar drew his attention to the box of coins sent by Sartaj. The head priest said, 'We take as much as we need. Thank the ruler and tell him there is no need now.'

'One more matter which needs to be resolved … that is the case of a head of the palace guard who came here to take the standard back in 1876.'

'Ah yes, he came here with a group of soldiers and in the English King's name demanded the return of the *chatri*. My predecessor at that time who was fiery tempered felt angered by the demand. The English captain warned him of his right to enter and seize. The Satrangi had prepared for a large skirmish, and that is it what it turned out to be. Many men were killed. With the Satrangi outnumbering the patrol, there was not much of a chance for any of the attackers, including the palace guard chief. He died in the desert … the spot is marked by a tablet. We have preserved two spots, one for the British captain and one for the chief of the palace guard.'

He took them to the spot where Sameera's ancestor had died. She uttered a brief prayer and decided to return the following year to put up a commemoration stone.

Later, with digital lenses focused on her against the backdrop of Amarpali Temple, Sameera introduced her account of the Satrangi Desert expedition to the world: 'This is the stuff dreams, if not legends, are made of – an unchartered desert, an undiscovered temple, a lost tribe, a feud lasting over ten centuries over a religious symbol, a princely state and a missing British Indian army patrol of Victorian vintage ...'

It was time to head back. The priest in appreciation of all that had been achieved, cut a piece from the alam which said 'Allah hu ...' and asked Meheryar to give it to the ruler, along with vats of honey, dried fruit, luscious lotus like pods, and a sweeter than maple like syrup.

The news about the discovery published by Sameera's newspaper and telecast simultaneously by Tasveer-e-Watan stirred up the entire nation, nay the entire world. The incident created waves greater than anyone could have foreseen. Every foreign newsman of worth seemed to land in the port city. All flights and other means of transport to Deriabad were booked. To spare the Satrangis the unwelcome publicity that would have blown their cover, the government arranged special air tours from Deriabad for flying around the site of the Amarpali Temple six times daily in order to provide a bird's eye view of the setting. Feet on the ground were prohibited. Interviews with the head priest facilitated by an interpreter were allowed on radiotelephone for limited durations.

Coverage of Deriabad palace, fragments of the standard and individuals including the nawab, Meheryar, Sameera, Rabby and Kamal who had provided the human element – reached worldwide audiences.

The journey had left its mark on the travellers. Meheryar and Sameera would marry. The equation had changed for Rabby and Kamal too.

'And they all lived happily ever after,' Behr-e-Karam said. 'Isn't that how adventure tales of princes and princesses are supposed to end?'

## Parting words from the vault

'There is something unreal about recent happenings,' Greybeard said.

'Unbelievable, the standard found draped over the dome of a Hindu temple,' said Curiouso.

Shocking, the lie that was put out about it,' Fussy Farhad said.

'Please,' Sufi Saeen said, 'do we have to belabour that again.'

'Everyone is entitled to some mistakes. I'm sure all of us have dark secrets which we haven't owned up to,' Artful Arbab said.

'It's about time for Steadfast Shahryar to awaken and take stock of what his offspring have been doing,' Grumbles said.

'Imagine a princess being shot by a commoner on a political matter,' said Curiouso.

'This is not the Deriabad I knew,' said Canny Kamran.

'But this is the Deriabad that will endure,' said Greybeard.

'Are you saying that because they have found the alam?' asked Curiouso.

'Not just on account of the alam… but, because the Umranis have found themselves,' said Greybeard. 'They have come together as a family.'

'A family!' murmured puzzled ancestors.

'How commonplace for royalty!' remarked Fussy Farhad.

'Whatever they do up there,' the Eldest Elder said, 'it will always be Deriabad … our Deriabad … because we are a part of the soil of the city.'

\* \* \* \* \* \*

Printed in the United States
By Bookmasters